DAYLIGHT SLAVERY

BY LEE KNAFA

First published in Great Britain in 2022

Cover design: Bodhi Design - www.bodhi-design.co.uk
Editing: Matthew McKeown - www.liverpool-literary.agency

ISBN print: 978-1-9993005-4-8
ISBN eBook: 978-1-9993005-5-5

Lee Knafa
The Liverpool Literary Agency

For Irene.

PROLOGUE

Kwento stood at his grandson's small, thatched bedroom window, trying to stare out into the blue blackness of the night. He rubbed away the condensation and then peered through the hole he had made with his sleeve. There was a chill and a dampness in the air around the open farmland, a far cry from the arid, open plains of the African savanna, a place that he still loved dearly and missed with a heavy heart, even after all these years.

He remembered it like it was yesterday, plucking the large, round oranges from low-hanging fruit trees and eating the sweet, sweet guavas and mangos that were in plenty. He had only to close his eyes for a brief moment to feel the hot, white sand between his toes, and the cooling deep-blue sea water rushing over his tiny brown feet, these dreams and memories now all he had left to comfort him.

Little Ben, his grandson, was sitting up in bed feeling very restless, showing no sign of wanting to go to sleep.

'I think it's going to rain tonight,' Kwento said with a yawn, before turning to face ben. 'The clouds look dark and angry.'

'I'm cold, Granddad,' Ben grumbled.

'Well then,' Kwento smiled warmly, 'let's get you tucked in smartly.'

'Will you read me a story, Granddad?' Ben asked.

'Oh, sweet Ben, there are no more stories to read to you.'

'Please, Granddad.'

'I must have read every book in the house to you twice already.'

'Tell me a story, then.'

The boy looked probingly into his grandfather's eyes, and Kwento let out a defeated sigh.

'If I tell you a story, you must promise to go straight to sleep, OK?'

'OK.'

Kwento sat down on the bed, and gently guided Ben's head down onto the pillow.

'Now, the story I'm about to tell you is going to be called Daylight Slavery,' he said. 'It goes way back to when I was only eight years old, still living in my village in Nigeria.'

'Nigeria? Where's that?'

'It's a country far, far away from here, down in Africa. Now, are you ready to hear my story?'

'Yeth,' Ben lisped enthusiastically, through the wide gap in his teeth.

'Well, one bright, sunny morning, my eldest brother Obi shook me awake. "Come on, sleepy head, it's time," he said to me. "Time for what?" I asked. "Time for you to become a man," he grinned. "But I don't want to become a man," I protested, "I'm happy the way I am, thank you very much." You're laughing, but this is what happened. Anyway, "You must come with me now because it is our father's wish," Obi insisted, "and you don't want to disobey father, do you?"'

'What did you do, Granddad?' Ben asked, sitting bolt upright again, eyes wide as he gazed up in wonder.

'I had to obey my father, what else could I do? So, I got dressed as quickly as I could, and then followed Obi deep into the pale-orange African outback, where we met up with the other youths of our tribe.'

'What was your tribe called?'

'We are called the Igbo people, and we have lived on the land since ages past. We are wealthy and well respected by all the other tribes in the region. Now, shall I continue with the story?'

'Yeth please.'

'I was taken to a small clearing deep in the bush, and made to stand in the centre armed only with a single long, thin spear. Ahead of me lay the tall, brown waving grass, interspersed by trees, and when I looked back, I could see my brother and the other boys standing well back, as if waiting for something to happen. My throat was dry, my palms became sweaty, and then, suddenly, I heard something coming towards me. The tops of the long grass parted, waving like long ears of wheat in a farmer's field. I was afraid, not knowing what was approaching. Was it a beast, or was it something even worse? There had been recent reports of slavers marauding around the local villages, so I wondered if that's what I would be facing, but then I heard the pounding of hooves getting nearer and nearer, beating the ground in time with the beats of my heart, harder and harder, louder and louder, nearer and nearer.'

'What are slavers, Granddad?'

'Slavers are very bad people, but thankfully, you will never have to meet them in your lifetime.'

'What happened next?'

'Well, I pointed my weapon, and waited to see what sort of beast would appear out of the long, thick bush, and I didn't have to wait long, I can tell you. The reeds gave way, and before me was the most hideous sight I'd ever seen.'

Ben pulled the covers up under his chin, holding them there tightly.

'It was large, brown and bloated, with a face like the devil himself,' Kwento went on. 'Its eyes were red and slanted, its tusks sharp as razors, pointed towards the heavens, and its flat, round pink snout puffed out long sprays of grey steam, like a locomotive engine.'

'What was it?'

'A wild boar, of course, and he was looking very angry.'

'What did you do?'

'The only thing that I could do. I stood my ground, raised my spear and stared back into its blood red eyes. This wasn't enough, though, for the beast was determined, and now heading straight for me. The pride of our nation rested on the outcome of this very moment, this very minute. Young boys just like me had stood in that very same place and done that very same thing over and over again, so why should this time be any different? Anyway, I'd made my decision.'

'Did you kill it, Granddad?' Ben croaked.

'I'm afraid not, Master Ben,' Kwento chuckled. 'I dropped my spear and ran away as fast as my legs would carry me.'

They both howled with laughter, as Kwento tickled Ben's ribs.

'Come along now,' he tucked Ben under the covers, 'it's bedtime for you, young man.'

'What's all this noise?' Polly, Kwento's wife, asked sternly, appearing in the doorway. 'Ben should be asleep by now.'

'I'm sorry, my dearest,' Kwento said, 'it's quite my fault.'

'Granddad told me a story about Africa and the beast,' Ben

beamed. 'It was very scary, but I liked it.'

'I'll have no more talk of Africa,' Polly ordered, 'and you should know better, Granddad.'

She joined Kwento in kissing Ben on the forehead and wishing him goodnight, before dousing the light and closing the bedroom door. They then both entered their small back parlour and sat down together.

It was the winter of 1888 in , Liverpool, the same year that Brazil announced the complete abolition of slavery, and Kwento, a former slave turned free man, had seen some remarkable changes in the town since his first arrival at the Coburg dock back in 1827. He felt that there was still plenty of room for improvement, however, especially when it came to attitudes towards race, as while a small minority of locals were beginning to tolerate the idea of mixed marriage, it must be said that the majority did not. This would often lead to clashes between men and women, blacks and whites, as people vented their anger and outrage, but this would only strengthen the resolve of those entering into mixed marriages, which began to increase regardless. The white women from the inner city of Liverpool seemed to prefer the freeAfrican men over their white counterparts because they were often merchant seamen with steady incomes and would treat their women better, never beating or abusing them.

'You look tired,' Polly said.

'Yes, I do feel a little fatigued,' Kwento admitted.

'Well, I'm not surprised. You're eighty years old and acting like a little child, scaring young Ben like that, with wild stories of Africa.'

'I know, I know – you're right as always, my sweet, but it was fun to reminisce.'

'Why don't you come to bed?'

'No, I think I'll just sit here a little while longer.'

'Very well, I'll pour us a cup of nice strong, sweet tea.'

'With some delicious homemade macaroons?'

They shared a chuckle, as Polly leaned over and placed two cups and saucers down onto the small side table, and then poured the tea.

'I was wrong about that old battleaxe, you know,' she sighed.

'We both were,' he said.

'She looked after me that woman.

Polly reached down deep into her pocket and pulled out a crisp white handkerchief.

'I know,' Kwento said, as she wiped her eyes. 'I'll tell you what, why don't we raise our cups to her?'

'Yes, let's do that,' Polly smiled.

They raised and clinked their white bone China cups in salute.

'To Mrs Alsop,' Polly said.

'To Mrs Alsop,' Kwento echoed, 'and God bless her.'

They fell silent for a moment, as Kwento leaned back into his easy chair and glanced across at Polly, who seemed far away, deep in thought.

'Do you think she's still alive?' she eventually spoke.

'Who, Mrs Alsop? No, she's long dead, my dear.'

'No, silly, I meant Miss Sarah.'

Leaning forward in his chair, Kwento became visibly uncomfortable upon hearing that name; one that had not been said between them in a very long time.

'Didn't we promise never to talk about her, my dear?' he moved quickly to cut the subject dead.

'Yes, we did,' she acknowledged, 'but I still think about her.'

'Well, I don't.'

'She was beautiful, though. Much prettier than me.'

'That's enough now, darling, please. I'll have no more talk of that woman.'

'But she was beautiful.'

'After all these years, you still blame me, don't you?'

'Don't be absurd,' she spluttered, turning her face away.

Kwento blew the air out of his cheeks, and then placed his hands behind his head as he leaned back into his large, comfy chair again.

'I've put you through so much, my love,' he said, 'and for that, I'm truly sorry.'

'What are you talking about, you silly old fool?'

'I'm talking about when I asked you to marry me all those years ago. You could have said no, and God knows if you had, I wouldn't have blamed you, but you said yes.'

'Of course I said yes,' she whispered gently, taking his hand in hers.

'You've had to put up with such a lot, my dear sweet Polly, raising our children whilst suffering constant racial abuse. It hurt me deeply when you used to come home after picking up the children from school, and tell me that some woman had just walked up to you and spat in your face, and called you a nigger lover. Thankfully, that sort of thing doesn't happen to you as often nowadays, since the children are all grown up and no longer go to school, but it was horrible when it did happen,' he let out a long sigh. 'I'd have to sit there and watch as you tried not to cry in front of me and the kids. Most women would have simply given up and walked away, but not you, not my Polly. You never complained, not once. You just did the best you could under the most difficult of circumstances, and that's why I love you so much, woman.'

'And I love you,' she gushed. 'I would do it all over again if I had to. I can still see you standing there like it was yesterday. You were stood in that old dark-grey kitchen with Mr Strome at your side, all rags and bones, but even then, I could see that you were handsome and exotic. I knew instantly that you were the one for me, even though, in reality, you were in love with Miss Sarah.'

'Now, that's just not true and you know it,' Kwento said firmly. 'Best not to talk about her, my dear.'

'Oh, I didn't say it to make you feel bad, my love. You've been a damn good husband and father. You gave me two beautiful children, and they have given us three gorgeous grandchildren. For that, you should be very proud.'

'Dearest Polly, know this. You've always been the love of my life. I loved you back then, I still love you now, and I will continue to love you until my last breath.'

Polly's bottom lip began to tremble slightly, and she had to steel herself as she began to well up with emotion before quickly switching back to the old matriarch, a shield that she had had to build up over the course of a long, difficult life.

'Don't go getting all soppy on me,' she coughed a little, as she fought to regain her composure, 'you old coot.'

They both laughed before moving towards each other and embracing.

'Anyway, we survived everything that they had to throw at us,' he said. 'They told you to forget about me – they said that I was to be shipped back to America, but you didn't listen. They said that you would never see me again, but you simply ignored them. You're a remarkable woman, Polly Holmes, do you know that?'

He recalled aloud how, when they were married at the registry office, the registrar could neither pronounce nor write his surname, and so took it upon himself to furnish Kwento with the name John

Thomas. Polly was furious at this, as she knew that this was a derogatory term that referred to a gentleman's privates, and she demanded that the registrar officially change it to Mr Kwento Holmes.

'Oh, stop it, you'll have me weeping in a minute,' she blushed. 'Why don't you come to bed, my love.'

'I think I'll just have a minute in this chair, if it's all the same to you,' he yawned.

'You do what you want. I'm off to bed.'

She closed the parlour door firmly behind her, and Kwento smiled as he closed his eyes and began to drift off. Telling his story to little Ben earlier had triggered something deep within his memory, and although he might have given his grandson a fictional account of his early years back home in Africa, the story had still brought back many of the horrid and vivid images that he had tried so very hard to forget. Now, all these years later, as he passed into slumber, he was beginning to resurrect the true version of what had really happened to him.

PART ONE

DREAMS OF AFRICA

THE IGALA KINGDOM, SOMEWHERE ON THE BANKS OF THE RIVER NIGER, 1820

It was a day like any other day, warm and sunny, and Ifeoma, Kwento's mother, was preparing the afternoon meal. She peeled and pounded the yam, diced the yuca root and mashed it into a stiff batter, before rolling the fufu into small, neat round balls, ready for the fish stew that was the family's favourite. She then instructed twelve-year-old Kwento to go with his elder brother Obi to fetch some kindling for the cooking fire.

Kwento went with his brother, and together they collected as much kindling as they could carry. Ifeoma also suggested that once Kwento returned with the kindling, he should go down to the riverbank to spear some catfish, but Obi was not comfortable with the idea of his little brother going alone, and offered to accompany him. Ifeoma flatly refused, however, insisting that Obi was needed at home, and arguing that Kwento was big enough to look after himself. As much as he had disagreed with his mother, and feared for his younger brother's safety, Obi dared not overrule her decision, no matter how big he was himself, and so he had to accept that there was nothing else for it.

Ifeoma had been the strong head of the household ever since the death of her husband ten years ago, after he was gored in the belly by a wild beast while out on the hunt. She had worked hard to raise her two sons as a single parent, something that she was very proud of, and everyone in the village would comment on how well-mannered and courteous the boys were, especially towards their elders. Kwento had grown up never really knowing his father, having only shadowy memories of him, and he wished dearly that he could have spent more time with him. It was for this reason that Kwento envied his brother, as from his point of view, Obi had enjoyed the best years of their father.

Kwento would often play tricks on his brother, such as pretending to fall down and hurt himself, only to then suddenly spring to his feet and run off when Obi stooped to tend to him; or setting homemade traps deep within the vast African bush, to frighten or ensnare him during their long walks. Although it was all done in jest, there was also a little bit of resentment behind it, stemming from Kwento's jealousy over the relationship Obi had had with their father. However, this is not to say that Kwento didn't love his brother, or that he would have ever wanted any real harm to come to him.

Ifeoma handed Kwento a large woven basket and a long spear, and sent him down to a riverbank located just a short distance from the family home. She told him that he was to spear as many fish as he could and then bring them back at once, blissfully unaware that as she issued these instructions, she was speaking to her dear, sweet boy for the last time. It was a day that would haunt her to her dying breath, as she never forgave herself for not listening when Obi made the case that Kwento was too young to be allowed to go down to the riverbank alone.

An hour later, Kwento had only managed to spear one large catfish for the stew, and he was felling quite low. I can't return home with such a poor catch, he thought, knowing that his mother would surely send him straight back out again if he turned up with a single measly fish. He decided to stay until he caught at least two more, but before he could go back into the water, he was approached by a man named Mustafa, who he recognised as being from a neighbouring village. Mustafa was marked by a diagonal scar across his face, left by a blow from a scimitar sword, which made him look quite menacing, and after smiling and gently teasing Kwento about his poor catch, he advised the boy to move further down the river, and offered to show him the best place to fish.

Eager to do a good job for his mother, Kwento followed Mustafa along the riverbank, feeling quite at ease with a man who he had seen many times in and around his village, and whose face and name were familiar to him.

They came to a stop near a grove of fig trees, and Mustafa pointed to a spot that he said was the best place for Catfish. Oblivious to any potential danger, Kwento crept forward towards the water's edge, only to be ambushed by a group of men, who bound and gagged the boy before roughly throwing him atop Mustafa's beautiful black Arab stallion. In what seemed the blink of an eye, they were galloping hard for the slavers' port of Calabar, on the tip of the Niger Delta, where despite the fact that slavery had been officially abolished in 1807, the trade was still alive and flourishing on the African Gold and Ivory coasts, which would continue to be the case well into the late 1830s and beyond.

Kwento had initially believed that he must have just happened to find himself in the wrong place at the wrong time, the victim of a simple misunderstanding, not realising that he had been deliberately kidnapped by Mustafa, due to a serious shortage of criminals and miscreants that normally filled the putrid bellies of the slavers' ships. Mustafa was a man with no morals or scruples to speak of, who only viewed people as pieces of meat to be traded for money. Kwento, on the other hand, was born into a good family, and should have been untouchable by his society's standards, free to travel wherever he pleased, but Mustafa knew that Kwento's family had recently converted to Christianity, which meant that as far as he was concerned, the boy was now fair game.

It was a full day's ride at the gallop to the old port of Calabar, during which Kwento was unseated several times from Mustafa's noble black horse, hurting himself in the process. Thus, Mustafa was forced to release Kwento from his bonds, allowing him to ride with him upright under strict instructions to hold on firmly to his captor's waist.

'Why are you doing this to me?' Kwento worked up the courage to ask.

'It's nothing personal, my little friend,' Mustafa answered. 'Just business.'

'Business?'

'Yes, business. The world around us is changing, and we must change with it. It's survival of the fittest, and I have no intention of being taken as a slave myself, do you understand?'

'No, Mustafa, I do not.'

'I will try to explain it to you. Some time ago, we were warned that a raid was about to take place on our village, but we chose to ignore this warning, and then they came – in the night, no less.'

'Who came in the night?'

'The slavers, of course. I managed to fight them off and escape, but not before they took my two brothers and most of my friends. It was at this moment I decided that no matter what I had to do, I was never going to be enslaved. I was always going to be a free man.

'By becoming a slaver yourself?'

'That is correct, yes. I do it to keep the beasts away from the door. You're far too young to understand this now, but one day you will know why I do what I do.'

Ironically, despite all his wheeling and dealing in his bid to remain a free man, Mustafa would eventually be trapped by white slavers and sent to the West Indies, never to be seen again.

'What will happen to me?' Kwento asked fearfully.

'Once we arrive in Calabar, you will be sold to the tally man, and then that's that. Behave yourself, and no harm will come to you. You have my word.'

'I won't give you any trouble, Mustafa. I promise.'

'That is good to hear, my little friend.

'What will happen once I'm sold?'

'You will be taken by longboat along the coast, and then handed over to the white man. What happens to you after that, I've no idea. Now, be quiet. We have a long journey ahead of us.'

Night had fallen by the time they reached the busy port, but although it was late in the evening, the place was still bustling with activity. Mustafa rode up to an old grey, weather-beaten colonial tent and dismounted, before taking Kwento by the arm and leading him inside, where he was introduced to the old black tally man, who was sucking hard on a homemade wooden pipe.

'What do we have here?' The tally man asked.

'A boy from my neighbouring village,' Mustafa said.

'Hunting so close to home, and taking such a young child?' the tally man raised his eyebrows. 'I presume business must be bad, eh?'

'That's not your concern,' Mustafa grunted. 'Just tell me what he's worth, and I will be on my way.'

The tally man pulled on his pipe a moment, and then, with a lazy arm, pointed to four bags of grain on the floor.

'What's this?' Mustafa shouted furiously. 'You know I only deal in hard currency. Bags of grain are of no use to me."

'Take it or leave it,' the old tally man shrugged his shoulders, and began slowly tipping out the ash from his pipe. 'It's all I have.'

'You must be joking. I have men waiting for their wages. I can't pay them with this.'

'Take it or–'

'Yes, yes, take it or leave it. I'll have to take it, God dammit.'

Mustafa turned to Kwento and placed his hand on his shoulder, looking directly into his face as he spoke.

'I know this won't mean much to you, but I wish you luck my little friend.'

Not for the first time, Kwento felt as though Mustafa was sending out mixed signals. On the one hand, he was coming across like he didn't really care for Kwento or his circumstance, seeing him only as a commodity to be traded, but at the same time, he appeared to feel sorry for him. It was all very confusing.

Mustafa tied the four sacks of grain to his horse and rode off into the night, leaving Kwento alone with the tally man. He was afraid, not knowing what the future would bring, and this sense of fear would resurrect itself many times throughout his proceeding years in captivity.

THE DOUGLAS

The very next morning after he was sold to the tally man, Kwento found himself being packed aboard a longboat with various other damned souls, and then taken on a seemingly endless journey along the infamous Gold and Ivory coasts to Senegal, where he was transferred onto the Douglas, a two-masted brigantine that could hold up to two hundred slaves at once. This was a smaller, more manoeuvrable ship than the larger and heavier three-masted barquentines, which had the capacity to carry six hundred slaves, with the brigantine becoming the vessel of choice by the late seventeen-eighties, due to its ability to sail in shallow waters and dock at almost any coastal port.

The Douglas was captained by the cruel shipmaster John Howard and his first mate Mr Thomas Wales. Captain Howard, known to his crewmen as Flogger Howard, was a fifty-year-old ex-Royal Navy officer, who had been dismissed from the HMS Resolve five years earlier for the excessive flogging of a young navy rating, hence the nickname 'Flogger.' Captain Howard was portly in stature, but he had a healthy constitution despite his craggy, weather-beaten face and short, stubbly grey beard, that he often stroked when feeling nervous or sinking into deep thought, and though it is true to say that he did not personally flog the young recruit, he did order the two hundred lashes with the cat o' nine tails, resulting in the death of the young seaman who had committed the minor offence of falling asleep whilst on duty.

To hear some tell it, Howard had not always been a cruel man, but had gone through a drastic change in personality following the sudden death of his beloved young wife Florence, just two years before he took command of HMS Resolve. He could not accept Florence's untimely demise, which also served to compound his long-standing regret over never having fathered children, and all of this tragedy was enough to cause a once deeply religious man to lose his faith. Over time, he became consumed by bitterness and resentment, often being heard to cite the passing of his bride as evidence that there could be no God.

After the flogging incident, Howard believed that he would never again command a ship, but while this was true of naval vessels, he would later find his salvation in the Douglas.

First Mate Thomas Wales walked onto the deck and immediately approached Sam Pretty, the boatswain, who was watching as the slaves were slowly being filed along and loaded into the Douglas' hold.

'Report, Mr Pretty,' Wales said.

'This is the last of them to be loaded, sir,' Pretty replied. 'Two hundred in all.'

'Just make sure you look after them, Mr Pretty,' Wales said pointedly.

'Don't know what you mean, sir?'

'I mean you need to keep an eye on your men. They urinated in the slaves' drinking water on the last journey. This must not happen again, do you understand?'

'Oh, that was just the lads having a bit of fun with old darky is all, sir.'

'Do not let it happen again. The captain lost a lot of revenue on our last journey. The stock must arrive unspoilt, understand?'

'Aye, sir,' Pretty snarled, wiping his nose on his sleeve.

'Oh, and Mr Pretty…'

'Sir?'

'Do you think that maybe on this voyage, you could keep our stores and provisions dry?'

'Don't I always, sir?'

'On the last voyage, the millet and corn meal were mouldy. It made the slaves sick.'

'Surely, I can't be blamed if the ship springs a leak here and there, sir?'

'Nevertheless, try to be vigilant, Mr Pretty. Vigilance is the key.'

'Aye, sir.'

'Now, time for the final checks, don't you think?'

'All done, sir. All is well.'

'Well, no harm in going through them all one last time, just to be on the safe side, is there? Gaff sails, main sail, foresail and jibs?'

'All fine, sir,' Pretty grumbled.

'Rat lines, main mast, foremast and bowsprit?'

'All fine, sir.'

'Very good. Carry on, Mr Pretty.'

'Aye, sir.'

Kwento entered the gloomy, claustrophobic hold. It was an area normally reserved for things like palm oil and gunpowder, but it would be his new home for the following three months. Shadowy and cramped, its ceiling was so low, he had to stoop to move around, and with only two lanterns hanging at opposite ends of the cavernous space, a strange dark-orange glow was cast over the poor wretches that were packed in tightly together. Kwento found these new surroundings uncomfortable and oppressive, and being there made him feel very angry, since he had done nothing wrong and could not understand why he was being treated so harshly. His first impressions of the crew were not good, either. The white men were rude and aggressive, especially the short, stocky one with blonde, curly hair, who Kwento assumed to be their leader. This man had deliberately moved his foot forward to cause a slave to trip and fall to the floor, before turning and bowing to his crew, who duly began to clap and cheer.

Thick oak beams creaked, and the wooden bulkheads glistened with damp seawater that had penetrated through the tiny cracks, as Kwento sat himself down in the three feet and three inches of space that had been allocated to him. There was no straw bedding, just bare, wet floorboards, and he decided right there and then that he must try to escape, even if the odds were greatly stacked against him. He hated this vessel with a passion already, and was determined to gain his freedom by any means possible. He started to scan every inch of the hold, looking for a means of escape, but the only way out was the same way he had entered. It all seemed quite hopeless from his position, and he quickly gave up any notion of getting free. He was then approached by a pale, skinny crewman, who smiled as he manacled him to the rest of the harassed and depressed-looking inmates. This signalled that any hope of escape was practically impossible, a realisation that left Kwento with his head lowered and body slumped over, completely deflated, and it wouldn't be long before he could feel the gentle rocking motion of the ship, confirming that the journey was under way.

The air below decks was thick and hot, stifling and suffocating. His nostrils quickly filled with the stench of urine, vomit and faeces that still lingered from the ship's previous occupants, and Kwento could have sworn that he felt his heart break in two as it finally hit home that he would never see his homeland ever again. His immediate thoughts were with his family; he knew they would be out looking for him, and he worried for his mother.

How will she cope without her baby? he thought. And what about Obi?

His brother was to assume their father's role by training Kwento as a warrior, not that of any of it mattered now. His old life was gone, to be replaced by one of misery and subjugation, but as his spirits plummeted and he began to cry, he saw through his tears that it was only the males who were chained together, whereas the female slaves were free to wander around the hold and above decks. There was a good reason for this: the females would act as nurses, tending to the wounds caused by the constant chafing of the iron ankle restraints. They were also tasked with cleaning up human waste and preparing meals from the limited ingredients of rice, beans, millet, corn and dried biscuit, as well as doling out the precious single cup of fresh water that the slaves were entitled to each day.

In addition to their domestic duties, the female slaves were expected to function as comfort girls for the crew. Thus, it was not uncommon for a crew member to enter the hold and select the prettiest young maiden, before dragging her off screaming by the arm. Kwento would come to find this ritual to be most offensive, and vowed revenge against any crewman who participated, for little though he was, he still regarded himself as a young warrior, and

Obi had always impressed upon him that it was a warrior's duty to protect the females of the tribe.

Often, when the ships reached the Americas, the masters would be delighted to learn that some of the female passengers had fallen pregnant during the voyage, effectively giving them two slaves for the price of one. It was quite common for men and women to be born, live and die in slavery, although some of the slave girls would contract syphilis as a result of the many rapes they were subjected to, leaving them barren and childless, as well as dangerously infectious to future sexual partners. With this in mind, the masters would complain to the ship captains, demanding that they take greater care of their female stock, but this would typically fall upon deaf ears, as a captain's only priority was to deliver his cargo alive and sellable.

A slim, muscular, bald-headed young man next to Kwento gently nudged him in the ribs with his elbow.

'Do you speak English?' he whispered.

'A little,' Kwento replied, his small voice barely audible.

'Good, then you may be useful to us. Now, stop crying. I'm going to look after you. My name is Baku, what is yours?'

'Kwento.'

'Pleased to meet you, Kwento. What tribe are you from?'

'The Igbo.'

'Ah, Igbo,' Baku smiled. 'I'm Yoruba. I know there have been tensions between our peoples in the past, but I will look after you, OK?'

'OK.'

'I'm told that life on the white man's boat can be very harsh, but stick by me and you'll be alright. By the way, who trapped you?'

'A man called Mustafa.'

'The traders are the worst,' Baku shook his head. 'They have no heart, only passion for the money.'

'I was going to be trained as a warrior by my older brother Obi, but Mustafa has robbed me of all that now.'

'No, he has not. I will train you. Now, who taught you to speak English?'

'The white missionaries.'

'That's good, but you must never let the white man know this, do you understand?'

'You mean, you don't want me to speak in his tongue?'

'I mean that I don't want you to speak to him in his tongue. The white man will speak freely if he thinks you don't understand him, and perhaps reveal some of his secrets – secrets that may give us important information and help us to escape, understand?'

'Yes, Baku.'

'Never trust the white man. He will always try to trick you, but if you stay alert then maybe, just maybe, you will survive all of this. There are many different tribes and many different languages down here, which is why we always try to communicate with each other in English, understand?'

'Yes, Baku.'

'Look around you,' Baku made a sweeping gesture with his arm. 'We have Gbe, Akan, Wolof, Chamba, Igbo and Yoruba all in one place, but down here, there is only one tribe, the slave tribe. Whilst you are onboard this vessel, you will always regard these people as your family, understand?'

'Yes, Baku.'

'See that young man over there?' Baku led Kwento's gaze with a pointed finger. 'His name is Akin. He, too, speaks in the white man's tongue, and if anything should happen to me, he will be the one to look after you, understand?'

'Yes, Baku.'

'He is Yoruba, like me. We got to know each other whilst on the narrow boat to Senegal. He's a fierce warrior, and has sworn to help me in my struggle for freedom.'

Kwento glanced over at Akin, who waved back with a huge grin on his face. It was a laudable attempt at trying to help the boy feel at ease, but it was going to take more than a smile and a wave to make this situation seem in any way bearable.

'I just want to go home,' Kwento blubbed. 'I miss my mother. I just want to go home!'

'And you will go home,' Baku said, placing a reassuring arm around the boy's shoulder. 'For the time being, look upon us as your new adopted family. We're going to look after you until we can return you to your mother.'

'You really think I'll see her again?'

'Absolutely! I have a plan that will get us all back to Africa, trust me. All will be revealed in due course, but for now, the best thing you can do is try to get some rest and save your strength. We will continue with your lessons tomorrow, little warrior.'

'Lessons?'

'Yes, life lessons.'

'I don't understand.'

'You will,' Baku winked.

Kwento tried to follow Baku's advice and make himself as comfortable as possible, leaning back and placing his head against the damp wooden bulkhead, but despite his best efforts to relax, his mind raced with what ifs.

What if I hadn't gone down to the riverbank alone? he thought. Would all this have happened? What if I had caught more than one

Catfish? Would I have returned home without running into that heartless Mustafa?

Eventually, he told himself that what was done was done, leaving him with no option but to prepare for the future, for good or bad, until the time came where he could return to his family.

Somehow, he managed to drift off, and was suddenly transported back home with his mother and brother, where he sat near the open fire, watching as she placed vegetables into the large black cooking pot. It felt good to once again be surrounded by the people he loved most and to feel the warmth of his mother, which gave him a sense of safety that he hadn't felt since his encounter with Mustafa at the riverbank. The sun was high and bright, and the orange trees swayed gently back and forth as Kwento stood to help his mother wash clothes by rubbing them against the big grey rocks, before helping her lay them out neatly in the sun to dry.

Obi split a large mango and handed one half to his mother and the other to Kwento, to help cool them down, and then he picked up a spear and began to perform an old warrior dance, badly. This made Kwento and his mother clap and giggle, drawing the attention of neighbours who decided to join in the fun and sat down alongside them, clapping along to Obi's awkward, jerky movements and encouraging him to jump higher and higher. It all became too much for young Kwento as, no longer able to contain himself, he joined his brother in the crudely-drawn battle circle and started jumping up and down, kicking up the dry orange dust. This delighted the boys' mother, who shouted and whistled loudly, but above all the cheers and claps, Kwento could hear a dull, foreboding thumping sound in the distance, which was getting closer and louder by the second.

Turning his head in the direction of the sound, Kwento could see a large dust cloud appearing on the horizon, out of which a group of fierce black stallions came galloping, with tall riders in long, starched white robes and thick white turbans, sending everyone running off in different directions in a screaming panic. Confused, Kwento was unable to process what was happening at first, but as the horde got closer, he realised that one of the leading outriders was none other than Mustafa, followed closely by his bandits, as it dawned on him that this was a raiding party in search of fresh victims for the slave ships.

Obi fought bravely, spear in hand, but he was no match for the rider who cut him down with a single blow from his razor-sharp scimitar. His mother was next, and as the Arab mare approached, she shouted at Kwento to run for his life, before being scooped up and swung over the back of the great black horse and whisked away at speed, leaving Kwento alone and crying.

As the dust finally settled, he felt the ground vibrate underneath his feet, as the unmistakable sound of hooves hammering against the floor came up fast from behind. He turned quickly to find a face marked by a diagonal scar bearing down upon him, and then, in one swift motion, Mustafa plucked him up like a weed from a flowerbed and rode off into the distance. Kwento kicked and screamed until, suddenly, there was a loud crack followed by a broad shaft of white light that shone down so brightly, it forced him to shield his eyes as he just about made out two blurred figures descending into the gloomy, dank hold. As they drew nearer, he recognised them as Thomas Wales and Sam Pretty.

The two men seemed to be searching for something or someone in particular, going from slave to slave, kicking each one as they went, and it occurred to Kwento that while Thomas Wales appeared to follow Captain Howard's instructions to the letter, often coming across as quite cold towards to the slaves, he had also been known to show kindness and affection towards Dara, one of the slave girls.

Wales stopped in front of Kwento, before leaning over and pointing a thick, grubby finger at him.

'Here he is, Mr Pretty,' Wales smirked. 'My little Brown Berry. Let's be having you, my little piccaninny.'

Pretty, who was best described by his own men as having blond curly hair and black curly teeth, was a thickset man with a permanent five o'clock shadow, who always seemed to look tired. He wore a black patch over his left eye, from under which a thin purple scare ran down the left side of his cheek, having reportedly been left by a blow from a cutlass. He was short in stature, which might have explained his apparent inferiority complex, and he had immediately struck Kwento as cruel and sadistic, encouraging the boy to keep a fearful distance. The boatswain would often tell anyone who asked, or who he thought would be bothered to listen, that the scar was an old battle wound, but the truth was that this so-called 'battle' was really just a brawl in a house of ill-repute. He was an odious character with little self-respect, a usurper spawned from the cesspit of life. He had been charged with sodomising a naval rating in his previous job, and was due to receive the maximum one thousand lashes before he was spirited away by his equally unsavoury cohorts.

Kwento winced as he was unshackled and jerked up roughly onto his feet.

'You're pretty, pretty, aren't ya?' Pretty said through his black pitted teeth, staring Kwento in the face.

'Leave the boy alone,' Wales snapped. 'He's for the Captain he is.'

'Yes, leave the boy alone,' Baku echoed breaking his own rule never to speak English in front of the crew.

At this, Pretty quickly produced his whip and began to lash Baku across his head and shoulders repeatedly.

'Shut your black face,' he roared, 'or you'll get some more of this.'

Kwento's heart quickened, his palms dampened and his throat became dry, as he was hit by the realisation that his worst nightmare was about to begin. It was obvious to him that he had been selected as the captain's comforter, a fate that he could do nothing to avoid as Wales and Pretty marched him up onto the deck and stood him before Howard himself, who gave a simple nod of the head instructing Wales to push the boy towards his quarters, located on the aft quarterdeck.

Inside the captain's cabin, Pretty chained Kwento to the bulkhead and ordered him to await his master. He didn't have to wait long.

Standing rooted to the spot, filled with trepidation, the only saving grace Kwento could think of was that these quarters were nothing short of roomy in comparison to down below. The ceiling was high, adorned with many hanging lanterns swaying gently in motion with the ship, and there was plenty of daylight entering through the massive glass windows situated behind the captain's desk. There was also a pleasant fragrance permeating the air, a product of the slow-burning incense sticks that were placed in each corner of the room.

As it happened, Kwento need not have worried about Howard's intent, as the captain had no designs on using him as anything other than a personal servant. If anything, the boy had been lucky to be chosen for the prized position of valet, or cabin boy, but he still did not like or trust Howard, viewing him as a significant cog in the machine that had turned his life upside down. In spite of his feelings, however, as time wore on, Kwento would become popular with the crew, often entertaining them on deck by dancing a jig to fiddle and drum, though in his own mind, this was only a façade, a mere distraction, to keep his enemies close. He might have been young, but he was nobody's fool; his mother had schooled him well.

Although things were generally going as well as could be expected for Kwento, his heart remained heavy due to the realisation that he had lost Baku as his protector.

How could he possibly help me if he's manacled below deck and I'm up here? he thought, seeing the young man who reminded him so much of his brother in his mind's eye. Baku looked to be around the same age as Obi, in his late teens or early twenties, and was similarly tall and muscular, with a slim, noble face. *It must have taken many hunters to bring him down. He is very brave, always looking his captor's dead in the eye. He must have killed many wild boar with his bare hands.*

He was pulled from his reverie by the sound of the cabin's small, brown oak door creaking open, as Captain Howard stooped to enter the room before standing upright in front of him.

'Do you speak English?' Howard asked, but got no answer. 'Hmm, I'll take that as a no.'

'He's a pure savage, sir,' Wales laughed, observing the scene from the doorway. 'You'll get nothing out of that one.'

'Does he have a name?'

'No, sir, but I've taken the liberty of naming him Brown Berry, if that's alright with you, sir?'

'Brown Berry it is,' Howard smiled wryly. 'Now, Brown Berry, your duties will include washing and ironing my clothes, helping Cook prepare my meals and keeping this place clean and tidy. In short, you will be my dog's body. Do you understand?'

Kwento simply stared back at him blankly.

'Um, he doesn't seem to understand me. Right then, your first duty is to pour myself and Mr Wales here some madeira.'

Howard gestured towards the flask that was sat on his table, as Pretty emerged from behind and crossed the room. The boatswain unchained Kwento and gave him a demonstration on how to pour the madeira into two large pewter tankards and then hand them out.

'I think this might work,' Howard nodded, accepting a drink from his new servant. 'Please leave us, Boatswain. Mr Wales and I have much to discuss.'

'Aye, sir,' Pretty bowed slightly, before exiting the cabin.

'What is the state of our provisions, Mr Wales?' Howard asked.

'Well, as long as we stay on course and incur no delays or deviations, we should have enough food and fresh drinking water to last us the rest of the journey, sir.'

'Very well, and what is the condition of the crew?'

'Riley, Baxter and Smith all have dysentery, and are laid up in their hammocks, sir.'

'And what of the rest?'

'The rest of the crew are suffering from either scurvy or syphilis, sir.'

'But they are still functional, correct?'

'Correct, sir.'

Kwento sensed an atmosphere in the room so thick, you could cut it with a knife. Captain Howard had done well to check his temper and, so far, he had not risen to Wales's tone or sarcasm, but all that was about to change very quickly.

'Very well,' the captain nodded. 'You know, Mr Wales, since we boarded the Douglas, you've seemed somewhat distracted.'

'Really, sir?' Wales feigned surprise at the statement.

'Yes, really, sir!'

'Well, now that you mention it, I was intending to speak with you once the opportunity presented itself.'

'There is something wrong, then?'

'I've decided that this will be my last voyage, sir.'

'Last voyage!' Howard cried, slamming his cup down on the desk. 'Last voyage! What the hell are you talking about?

'I've decided to retire, sir,' Wales said evenly.

'Retire? Retire? Explain yourself.'

'Just, um, personal reasons, sir.'

'You'll have to do better than that, Mr. Wales?'

'Very well, sir. Once we're back in England, it is my intention to take up a land-based position.'

'Land-based?' Howard shook his head in disbelief. 'Tell me, Mr Wales how long have you been at sea?'

'You know how long, sir.'

'Humour me.'

'Since I was a boy of fourteen, sir.'

'And now suddenly, after all this time, you just decide to quit without any further explanation. I find that very strange.'

'Well, there it is, sir.'

'There it is indeed! I'm sure I don't like your attitude, and I demand to know the real reason for your decision, for I don't buy this one for a second.'

'Very well, sir. As you know, I served on this ship under Captain Richards, long before you took command of it.'

'Your point being?'

'Simply that I am accustomed to the way in which Captain Richards ran a vessel.'

'Ah, now we're getting somewhere. Please continue, and spare me your attempts at diplomacy.'

'You treat your crew far too harshly,' Wales said, after a moment's hesitation. 'We lose men after every journey due to the almost daily beatings, not to mention the terrible food and conditions that lead to poor health, none of which seem to bother you in the slightest. I respect the fact that, as captain, you are within your rights to operate however you see fit, but I can tolerate it no longer. There, you asked for the real reason, and now you have it.'

'I appreciate your candour, Mr Wales, but may I remind you that this is a slave ship, not a luxury cruise vessel. Slaving is a serious business, and it must be run by serious people. Now, I'm not going to lie to you, it will be hard to replace such an experienced crewman as yourself, but know this. While you are under my command, you will carry out my orders to the letter, understood?'

'Of course, sir. May I be away?'

'Go about your business.'

'Aye, sir.'

Wales quickly downed the rest of his wine before turning and exiting the cabin in one swift motion.

Taking up a position on the afterdeck, Thomas Wales looked down the main beam of the ship and watched as the boatswain whipped his crew into action. The weather was turning for the worse, with dark grey clouds starting to form on the horizon, when a lone voice cried out from high up in the rigging.

'Vessel approaching from the east!'

At once, Wales extended his brass telescope and tried desperately to focus through the cracked, foggy lens. Sure enough, there was indeed a ship fast approaching, and it was not long before the first mate was joined by Captain Howard.

'What do you have for me, Mr Wales?'

'It would appear that we have a ship on a direct intercept course with us, sir.'

'Can you make out anything from this distance?'

'Yes, she's a square-rigged brigantine, sailing under a Portuguese flag.'

'Portuguese, you say?'

'Aye, sir.'

The sea was becoming choppy, and Howard clung to the taffrail to steady his balance as he walked along the short deck. He was clearly deep in thought, wearing a concerned look on his face, as he snatched the telescope and looked through it himself.

'Should we drop anchor, sir?' Wales asked.

'Certainly not.'

'What are your orders?'

'We stay the course, Mr Wales.'

'But we can't outrun her, sir. She's bearing down on us fast.'

'Stay the course and deploy snipers to the rigging.'

'Snipers? Are you expecting trouble, sir?'

'Possibly, Mr Wales. Possibly.'

'Do you suspect they could be pirates, sir?'

'There haven't been pirates on the high seas since seventeen-thirty, Mr Wales. Calm yourself – you'll frighten the crew.'

'I beg to differ, sir. I've heard that there are still regular skirmishes around the Caribbean islands.'

'We are nowhere near the Caribbean,' Howard growled. 'There are no pirates here, Mr Wales, I can assure you.'

'If they aren't pirates, what are they?'

'Opportunists, Mr Wales. Merely opportunists.'

'Isn't that the same thing, sir?'

'I'm not going to stand here and argue semantics,' Howard

bristled. 'Now, I want all able-bodied men armed to the teeth, and then give the order that they are to prepare to be boarded. If the Portuguese want this ship, they will have to fight for it.'

'Aye, sir.'

With the assistance of Sam Pretty, Wales handed out clubs, knives, axes and pistols to all crewmen, and stood ready as the opposing vessel pulled up alongside them with all four gun ports open, providing a terrifying sight for those who understood that the Douglas was no match for such an arsenal. Amid the growing tension, Wales could only hope that his captain had a sound plan in mind. He knew that they would only get one chance to strike, and if it went wrong, the consequences would not bear thinking about.

So, there are no pirates, eh? he thought, glancing at Howard with a barely-concealed smirk, before observing with some surprise that his fellow crewmen appeared strangely calm, all told. This gave him hope that maybe they were in with a chance should it come to direct conflict.

Kwento felt mixed emotions as he watched the scene unfold from the afterdeck. He was both fearful and excited at the same time, not to mention curious as to how the captain would react to this potentially threatening situation, and also how the white warriors would fare should it come to battle. He watched with great interest and anticipation as the captain of the Portuguese ship stood proudly on the middle deck with his hands cupped around his mouth, as if ready to shout something. The unexpected visitor was at least six-feet tall, with a thick mop of black curly hair and a matching bushy beard, and a cutlass and two pistols displayed on his wide, brown leather belt, all of which combined to create a very rough-and-ready appearance. He was met by Captain Howard, who also wore a cutlass and pistol, plus a dagger tucked neatly beneath his own leather belt, and as they stood in a silent standoff, the two men made for an impressive sight indeed.

'Permission to come aboard, captain,' the Portuguese hailed.

'Permission granted,' Howard replied, smiling confidently.

'Sir, what are you doing?' Wales asked, a hint of panic in his voice.

'Start smiling, Mr Wales,' Howard said through his teeth. 'We're all friends out here.'

'Fiends!' Wales exclaimed. 'The bastards want to kill us!'

'We don't know that for certain yet, Mr Wales. Just bear with me and play the game.'

'A very dangerous game, if I may say so, sir.'

As it turned out, Mr Wales need not have feared the outcome of this game, it being one that Captain Howard had played many times before in his role as a Royal Navy officer. To Howard, this was nothing more than an impromptu chess match, a game which, incidentally, he was very good at playing and winning. To hear him explain it, it was just a simple matter of guessing an opponent's next move before they had a chance to make it.

The Portuguese captain and his first officer were welcomed aboard, and there were lots of handshakes, nods and pleasantries before the guests were ushered inside Howard's cabin, where they were both offered a seat at his large oak table. It was at this point that the Portuguese captain seemed to become fascinated with Kwento, being unable to keep his eyes off him.

'You have a fine ship, Captain,' he said approvingly.

'Thank you, Captain…'

'Oh, forgive me. I am Captain Alvaro D'Argus, and this is my first officer Alberto Silva, at your service.'

'My name is Captain John Howard, and this is my first officer Mr

Thomas Wales. Pleased to meet you both.'

'Pleased to meet you, Mr Wales,' D'Argus nodded.

'Captain,' Wales returned the gesture.

'Interesting, I see that you have a black servant,' D'Argus observed.

'I thought everybody had one these days,' Howard said.

'Not everybody can afford one. They're very expensive, don't you know?'

'Oh? Anyway, Captain, how may we help you?'

'On the contrary, Captain Howard. It is I who has come to help you.'

'I wasn't aware that we were in need of any help.'

'Your ship appeared to be in distress, which is why we came rushing to your aid. The open seas can be a very cruel place, Captain,' D'Argus leaned forward. 'A very cruel place indeed.'

'I can assure you that there's nothing wrong with this vessel,' Howard smiled thinly.

'Very well. Perhaps it was simply a mistake on our part. So, where are you headed, Captain Howard?'

'For the Americas. May I ask your destination, sir?'

'We're on our way home.'

'And where would that be exactly?'

'Why, Portugal, of course. Did you not see our flag?'

'I did. It's just that you came in from the east.'

Howard was playing the game well, and was starting to turn up the heat on Captain D'Argus, who began to look a little flummoxed.

'That is correct,' the Portuguese said. 'We veered when we saw your vessel.

'Because you thought we were in distress?'

'Once again, you are correct. But tell me, Captain Howard, if your heading for the Americas, from whence did you set sail?'

It was the killer question that Howard was hoping D'Argus would not ask, and he had to be very careful and measured with his answer, not daring admit that he set sail from Africa, as that would mean the game was up for sure. He needed to knock D'Argus off course, as they would say in the navy, by coming up with a convincing diversion.

'Oh, please forgive my manners, Captain D'Argus,' he brought his hands up to his head, feigning embarrassment. 'May I offer you and your first officer a beverage?'

'Do you have Jamaican rum, Captain?' D'Argus asked, after a moment's consideration.

'Of course,' Howard beamed, 'all British vessels have Jamaican rum onboard.' He turned to Kwento. 'Brown Berry, rum for the captain and first officer.'

'Ah, Brown Berry, nice name,' D'Argus said, stroking his thick beard.

The Portuguese watched with darting snake eyes as Kwento began to pour the rum, and then suddenly gripped the boy by the wrist, holding him firm. Wales made a move towards D'Argus, but was first blocked by Silva, before Howard ordered his man to stand fast.

'May I ask what cargo you're carrying, Captain?' D'Argus asked.

'Oh, nothing of value, I'm afraid,' Howard coughed nervously.

At this, D'Argus slammed down his pewter tankard hard against the dark oak table, spilling the precious rum in every direction.

'Do not fence with me, sir!' he erupted. 'Are you carrying slaves?'

'Before we continue with this conversation,' Howard answered calmly, 'I would ask that you first release the boy.'

'Yes, yes, of course,' D'Argus grinned mischievously, as he

loosened his grip on Kwento and began patting him down, as if to straighten his clothing. 'Forgive me, Captain. I meant no harm, you understand?'

'Thank you, Mr D'Argus. Now, it's like I said. We have nothing of value here.'

'Oh, but I disagree. Slaves can be very valuable, if sold to the right buyer.'

'And I assume that you would know the right buyer, Captain D'Argus?'

'I would, which is why I intend to relieve you of your cargo, sir.'

Such a clear threat meant that this chess game had placed Captain Howard in check, and now he had to make a quick decision. At once, he decided to escalate the situation by springing to his feet and kicking back his chair, all in the same motion.

'And so it begins,' he growled, more than confident that he had the measure of this man, having figured that Captain D'Argus was not the sharpest tool in the box.

The two captains each drew their pistols and levelled them at the other's chests, leaving Kwento, Wales and Silva all standing rigid in the knowledge that their lives hung by a thread, as both Howard and D'Argus slowly danced the deadly waltz around the large oak table until they finally stopped face-to-face, staring down the barrels. Howard kept his eyes trained on D'Argus, and D'Argus watched Howard's trigger finger, swallowing hard as a thin bead of sweat began to trickle slowly down his forehead before dripping from his right eyebrow.

'This was never a rescue mission, was it, Captain D'Argus?'

'Oh no,' D'Argus said sarcastically, 'it would appear that you have seen right through me, Captain.'

'Yes, which is why I put snipers in the rigging before you had even set foot on my deck, and armed the rest of my crewmen to the teeth.'

Captain D'Argus stood in deep thought for a moment, rubbing his long, bushy black beard.

'Look, I'm not an unreasonable man,' he said, waving his pistol as though to emphasise the point. 'Maybe we can cut a deal.'

Howard was becoming convinced that he now had D'Argus exactly where he wanted him, breaking into a half-smile as he slowly lowered his weapon.

'Go on,' he said.

'Just give me the boy and any black bitches that you have in the hold, and I'll be aways,' D'Argus offered. What say you?'

'Don't listen to him, Captain,' Wales whispered. 'He'll take our cargo and then kill us anyway.'

Kwento held his breath as he looked across at Captain Howard, who seemed to be seriously considering D'Argus's offer.

'If you want this ship's cargo, Mr D'Argus, you will damned well have to fight for it,' Howard hissed.

'Don't be a fool, Captain,' D'Argus snarled. 'I have four cannons trained on your vessel.'

'That may be true, sir, but I suspect that you will not use them.'

'Oh? And what makes you so sure?'

'For one thing, your cannons are just above the water line, correct?'

'That is correct, yes.'

'Well, since the slaves are all chained below decks, if you fire on us, you will kill every one of them. In other words, you will walk away with nothing, so where do we go from here?'

'You're a very clever man, Captain Howard,' D'Argus allowed, 'but what's to stop me just blasting you out of the water anyway?'

'It's a gamble on my part, I'll admit. I'm gambling on you not wanting to waste ammunition, which could be put to better use in future encounters that may be lurking just around the corner.'

'And what you are gambling with is the lives of everyone onboard this ship, Captain. Do the right thing, and hand over the boy and the females.

'You will take them over my dead body, Mr D'Argus.'

'I don't like your tone, Captain. That is the sixth time you have referred to me as "Mr D'Argus," rather than Captain. I will have the respect that befits my rank!'

'You'll get no respect here,' Howard spat. 'You're a bandit, not a Captain, now get off my ship!'

'I will blow you out of the water!' D'Argus blazed. 'You will all die!'

'Do your worst, Mr D'Argus!'

Before D'Argus could reply, Silva took a step towards him and whispered something in his ear. D'Argos then thought for a moment before taking a deep breath and holstering his pistol.

'Keep your slaves and keep your damned ship,' he said. 'You're not worth fighting over. Come, Mr Silva, let's be aways while the day is still young. There's a vessel somewhere out there just waiting to be plundered.'

'Aye, sir,' Mr Silva nodded, his face a picture of relief.

As he followed his first officer out through the small cabin doorway, D'Argus suddenly stopped and turned on his heels, jabbing a pointed finger in Howard's direction.

'Watch your back,' he said darkly, 'for if we should meet again, Captain, I will not be so accommodating.'

Without a word, Captain Howard walked slowly around his large oak table and sat down. He then opened his logbook and pretended to write something in it before looking up at Captain D'Argus again.

'Are you still here?' he asked.

First Mate Thomas Wales was standing on the foredeck, looking out into the grey abyss. He could see that the weather was worsening, but his thoughts were with his wife, Mary, and their two children, Jack and Ruby, back home in Portsmouth. He had left for sea under a dark cloud, with Mary arguing that she was sick of worrying about him during these long voyages, and begging him to give it up in exchange for a safe land-based job. She confessed to suffering regular waking nightmares in which she would foresee his death, and after at first reminding her that he was a sailor when she had met and married him, he eventually relented and agreed, promising to make this his last tour. However, the truth was that the idea of spending more time at home filled him with trepidation, for he considered himself trapped in a loveless marriage, and relished the time away that his work afforded him. He could not imagine how he would survive in domesticity, and feared that he would end up being more like a lodger than a lover to his wife, the deep feelings that he once had had for her having long faded away, along with the passion that used to exist between him. They had stopped making love some time ago, and by this point, the relationship was so platonic that he had begun to consider Mary as something akin to a sister, rather than a wife to have and to hold.

As he leaned forward against the rail, Wales noticed Dr Green approaching. A fifty-two-year-old ex-Royal Navy surgeon, commonly known as the Butcher, Green had served on the Douglas since 1814, after being struck off by the Royal College of Surgeons following botched surgical procedures carried out whilst drunk. He was a tall, gaunt-looking individual, who appeared to be in need of a doctor himself.

'Are you alright, Mr Wales?' Green asked.

'Yes, I'm fine, thank you, Doctor,' Wales answered. 'I'm certainly not in need of any medical attention, if that's what you mean.'

'No, not at all. You just seem a little distracted.'

'I'm fine, thank you. Is there anything else?'

'No, no, just fancied a little chat, if you're not too busy, that is?'

'What's on your mind, Doctor?'

'Well, we've been at sea for six weeks now. We're halfway to the Americas.'

'Your point being?'

'My point is that we need to pay more attention to our cargo, Mr Wales.'

'By "cargo," I take it you're referring to the slaves?'

'Indeed, yes. You do care about them quite a bit, don't you?'

'My dear doctor, I have no feelings towards the Africans, good or bad. They're just livestock to me.'

'We both know that isn't true.'

'I'm sure I've no idea what you are talking about.'

'Everyone knows that you have feelings for Dara. It is obvious.'

'Oh, come off it. She's nothing more than a comforter. You of all people should know that. I never mix business with pleasure, sir.'

'If you say so, Mr Wales.'

'I do say so, Doctor. Not that it matters now anyway. I've informed the captain that this is to be my last voyage.'

'Your last voyage! What on earth are you talking about, man? You're an old sea dog – you couldn't possibly hope to function on land.'

'I made a promise to my wife, and it's one that I must keep.

Although, to be honest with you, Doctor, I've simply had enough besides.'

'I'll believe it when I see it, Mr Wales, but for now, back to business. After what happened on our last voyage, I am recommending improved medical treatment for both slaves and crewmen alike.'

'Better treatment?' Wales scoffed. 'The captain would never go for that. He's not the most compassionate of men, in case you hadn't noticed.'

'Be that as it may, we're losing far too much livestock to dysentery, typhus and yellow fever, and something has to be done, I tell you!'

'When did "the Butcher" develop such an acute sense of right and wrong?'

'When half the crew started dying, sir. We simply cannot continue to sustain these loses. Something has to be done, and done quickly.'

'So, what do you suggest?'

'Clean water for a start. Better sanitation, better food and fresh air for the slaves. They must be allowed up on deck.'

'The captain will never allow slaves on deck, Doctor.'

'Oh, and why not?'

'Risk of mutiny.'

'Mutiny! After six weeks at sea, stuffed in that stinking hold, they'd be lucky to stand upright, let alone riot! You must speak with the captain, Mr Wales.'

'I cannot do that, I'm sorry.'

'If not for the slaves, do it for your crew, man! On the last voyage, four sailors jumped ship at New Orleans because they couldn't face the journey back and they will do it again. At least allow them some basic treatment, like fresh vegetables or oranges and lemons to help with the scurvy.'

'May I remind you, Doctor, that this is a slave ship, not some kind of luxury pleasure vessel.'

'Very well, Mr Wales, have it your way, but do not blame me when we arrive in the Americas with all your crewmen dead, sir.'

'Storm!' a panicked voice cried out from the crow's nest. 'Storm coming in from the west!'

Wales shielded his eyes with his right hand as he looked out to sea. There was indeed a storm coming, and it was moving fast.

'Mr Pretty!' he bellowed at the top of his lungs. 'Drop the rigging and secure the decks! We're going to have to ride this one out, God dammit!'

'Aye, sir,' Pretty replied. 'Drop the rigging! Secure the decks!'

THE LONG, RUSTY NAIL

Kwento was trapped below decks. He had slipped a few scraps of food from the captain's plate into a muslin bag, and taken it down to his friend Baku at the exact moment when the storm was announced. It was not, however, the storm from above that posed the greatest threat, but rather the one raging around him that would have far greater consequences. The slaves were being rocked by the violent motion of the sea, which drenched them in falling ice water. Many were frightened and feared for their lives, while others were too sick to even care, and just continued to vomit all over themselves repeatedly.

As the seawater washed back and forth across the floor, it somehow managed to dislodge a long, rusty nail, which caught Baku's eye. He asked Kwento to bring it over to him, and began using it to pick away at his manacles.

'I have a plan,' he said, 'and once I'm free, I'm going to release all the other slaves. We have many warriors down here, so it should be easy enough to take over this vessel and turn us back towards home. All I need to know is, are you with me, little warrior?'

'I'm afraid, Baku,' Kwento trembled. 'What if we should fail? What will happen to us?'

'If we fail, they will just put us back in irons,' Baku smiled affectionately, rubbing Kwento's head. 'Don't be afraid, little warrior. Everything's going to be alright, but you must trust me.'

'I do trust you, Baku.'

Kwento's heart filled with joy in the belief that liberty and freedom were close at hand, and he began to imagine himself being back home with his mother and brother, not realising that Baku had just lied to him, albeit for a good reason. The slavery system was designed to strike fear and dread in any who dared consider rebellion, which meant that if their attempt was to fail, they could expect to be castrated or lynched, or in the most extreme cases, roasted alive or have gunpowder poured into their rectum and ignited. If the slave should flee his master and was later captured, he could sometimes expect to have his legs amputated.

'I think this lock is about to give way,' Baku grunted. 'I should be free of these things at any moment.' He pulled Kwento in close, before turning to address Akin in a low whisper. 'Now, listen up. Once you're free, I want you and Kwento to gather whatever materials you can from the hold.'

'Weapons?' Akin asked. 'There are no weapons here.'

'Use your imagination,' Baku said, revealing the rusty nail he was holding in the palm of his hand. 'There must be more of these lying around. If you find a loose board, pull it off and break it, and then make a dagger or spikes from the splinters. There's always something you can use.'

Suddenly, the hatches flew open, sending daylight and seawater crashing down onto the slaves huddled below, as Sam Pretty descended into the hold with a small bag of camphor under his nose to help mask the stench. He then set about checking for leaks while assessing the slaves' condition, and Baku quickly hid the nail in his hand as he watched the boatswain go from slave to slave, pulling on their chains.

Pretty was stopped dead in his tracks when he saw Kwento standing there, obviously confused as to why the boy was down below instead of up in the captain's quarters. He crouched down next to Kwento and snatched the bag of food, his face turning beetroot with anger as he quickly realised what was going on.

'Well, well, what do we have here, me pretty, pretty?' he said menacingly, seizing Kwento by the shoulders and shaking him violently. 'Been feeding all your black mates, eh? Well, you'll have to be punished for this, me little Brown Berry. You know that, don't you?'

Without needing to know this man personally, Kwento's instincts told him that he was in great danger, and he decided that he had no choice other than to break Baku's rule to never reveal to the white man that he could not only understand English, but also speak it.

'Please, sir,' he said pleadingly.

'Oh, it speaks the King's English,' Pretty said, looking around him in surprise. 'You're very tricksy, aren't ya, me brown berry?'

'Please don't hurt me, sir. I'm sorry.'

'Sorry, eh? Well, you will be sorry, boy. Come with me.'

'Leave him be!' Baku roared, from his place on the floor.

'Well, well, well,' Pretty laughed. 'Another who speaks the King's, eh?'

'Don't act so surprised, Pretty,' Baku said. 'You know I speak the King's.'

'Indeed,' Pretty nodded. 'Now, ready for another beating, are ya?'

The boatswain swaggered over to Baku and, placing his left hand under the slave's chin, lifted his head before bringing a fist down against his face with such force, it left blood on his knuckles. 'And what are you going to do about it, lying there chained to the fucking floor?'

Pretty smirked as he took Kwento by the arm and led him to the other side of the hold, where he shoved him behind a low wooden partition.

'Time for your punishment, me lad-o.'

He bent Kwento over, and although the boy fought wildly, he was soon tamed by the older man's much larger stocky frame.

'I'm going to teach you a lesson, pretty, pretty,' Pretty said, licking the saliva from his lips as he began to slowly unbuckle his broad, black leather belt. 'A lesson that you will never forget.'

As luck would have it, Baku had since managed to prise his manacles open with the long, rusty nail, and once free, he picked up a thick piece of timber and brought it down hard on the back of Pretty's head, sending him sprawling to the floor.

'Thank you, Baku,' Kwento wept, looking up at his saviour through teary eyes.

'It's OK, little warrior,' Baku said gently. 'Now, get yourself back to the captain's cabin and stay there. Say nothing of what has happened here, understand?'

'I understand,' Kwento nodded.

'Very good. Now, go quickly – quickly!'

Baku sat back down and started to replace his manacles, an action that both confused and enraged Akin.

'Baku, what the hell are you doing?' he protested. 'Now is the time to strike, whilst the storm is upon us!'

'Patience, my brother,' Baku replied calmly. 'This is not the right time.

'But we may never get another chance like this again!'

'No, we must wait. If we make a move now, we will be stopped. When they can't find the boatswain, they will come looking for him, and if they find us moving around freely, we will never make it out of here alive.'

'I still say we should attack now.'

'You'll just have to trust me, Akin. I have a plan.'

Meanwhile, Kwento had moved swiftly up and on to the deck, where he managed to enter the captain's cabin unnoticed. The storm had started to subside, and just as Baku predicted, it wasn't long before Captain Howard noticed that his boatswain was missing. A search party was sent to find Pretty, it being feared that he had been washed overboard, and once he was discovered lying unconscious on the floor of the hold, Howard ordered that all the slaves be brought up on deck as part of an immediate investigation.

Howard lined the slaves up on either side of the gaff sail, beneath the larger of the two masts, and paced up and down the lines with his hands behind his back. His face was flushed, and he looked very agitated.

'Whilst the storm was raging,' he began, 'someone took the opportunity to attack a member of the crew, fracturing his skull. Such behaviour will not be tolerated aboard this ship – order must be restored. Now, I will only ask once for the perpetrator to do the right thing and step forward to take their punishment.'

Nobody moved, prompting Howard to point to Dara, one of the young Igbo slave girls, before ordering a crewman to strip her naked and tie her to the mast. The crewman grinned as he carried out his orders, while Thomas Wales looked on in disbelief. His head was spinning with confusion, as he asked himself why, out of all the slave girls, Howard chose her.

Is he playing mind games with me? he wondered. If so, how does he know there is a connection between us?

He then recalled the conversation he had had with Dr Green on the foredeck. 'Everyone knows you have feelings for the slave girl,' the doctor had said, and if he knew, chances were that the captain would know, too.

Dara sobbed as she was dragged to the mast. Looking all around her with a dazed look on her face, she clearly didn't understand why she had been singled out when the captain knew that she had done nothing wrong. She was tall, slim and highly attractive, wearing large, hooped wooden earrings that complemented her short, tight, curly hair. Wales had initially taken her for his comfort, but had soon developed deep feelings for her; feelings that were very much reciprocated, and it was easy to see why she was attracted to him. Wearing his brown hair pulled back neatly in a ponytail, tied up in a short white ribbon, he was a handsome man indeed, with a chiselled jaw and a face that, unusual for a mariner of the time, he kept clean-shaven. Often, when they lay together, he would talk of plans to leave his wife and settle down with Dara in America. He intended to buy and then release her from her contract, after which they would spend the rest of their lives together in the new world.

Embarrassed, Dara raised her arms to protect her modesty, but the cruel sailor tied them back down by her sides, to further humiliate her, as Wales stepped forward with the cat o' nine tails and began to unfold the tarred braids of hemp, specifically designed to tear into the flesh and inflict maximum pain.

'Start with fifty lashes, Mr Wales,' Howard commanded.

'Fifty lashes, aye, sir.'

The atmosphere was heavy, the mood sombre, and Wales dared not look up, so wracked was he with guilt. He felt many eyes upon him as he unfurled the whip in preparation for a job that would have normally fallen to the boatswain, but as Sam Pretty remained laid-up in his bunk with a heavily-bandaged head, the responsibility was his. Indeed, whilst all this was going on, Pretty lay feeling sorry for himself below, cradling his bandaged head with one hand and clutching a sharp dagger in the other. His heart was filled with rage and his head was filled with anger, as his memory slowly began to return. He recalled catching sight of Baku just before he was struck over the head with a piece of timber, leaving him in no doubt as to the identity of his assailant. In his mind, he rehearsed over and over how he would plunge the dagger deep into Baku's black heart in revenge.

Nausea surged through Wale's churning stomach, as the secret knowledge that Dara was pregnant with his child flashed across his mind. He dangled the whip, feeling drained and helpless as he looked deep into her streaming eyes, for he dare not challenge the captain's orders, especially in public. He paused a moment, in the vain hope that the perpetrator would be compelled to reveal themselves, but when it became clear that nobody was going to step forward, he pulled back his right arm and, wearing a grimaced face, brought down the whip with all his might.

The witnesses gawked as they watched thin red lines appear across Dara's tight brown skin, and then gasped as the wounds began to weep slowly down her back. The girl let out bloodcurdling screams as she gripped the mast with both hands, at which point Baku moved to step out from the ranks.

'What the hell do you think you're doing?' Akin hissed, thrusting out an arm to block the way. 'No, I will take the beating. Without you to lead us, there will be no rebellion.'

'No, brother,' Baku met Akin's wide-eyed gaze, 'this is my burden.

Please, move aside.

'I won't let you do this,' Akin insisted.

'You're in charge now,' Baku put a hand on Akin's shoulder. 'Just promise me that you'll look after the little warrior.'

'What do you mean? You're talking like you're not coming back.'

'Freedom comes at a price, my brother. Look after the boy.' Baku turned to Kwento, and said to him in their native tongue, 'Gbe gun ki inu re dun [Live long and be happy],' as he shook his hand and secretly passed him the long, rusty nail.

Kwento's heart filled with dread. He knew something was very wrong, as this was the first time that Baku had spoken to him in anything other than English, and his worst fears were confirmed when his friend and protector walked towards the main mast and made himself ready to receive his punishment.

'Release the girl,' Howard ordered. 'It would appear that we have our culprit at last.'

'Aye, sir,' Wales said, his relief obvious.

Dara was swiftly replaced by Baku, who looked across at Kwento and winked, in an effort to reassure the boy that everything was going to be alright, before steeling himself ahead of what was to come. Kwento clenched his fists as his eyes burned red and filled with tears, fuelled by the thought that this was probably the last time they would see each other.'

'You're going to pay for this, my young black buck,' Howard smirked. 'Let's start with five hundred, Mr Wales.'

'Five hundred, aye, sir,' Wales nodded.

After three hundred lashes, Baku's back had opened up, his flesh raw and shredded, but he would not cry out, much to the annoyance of the captain. To the relief of the slaves, who had stood in complete silence throughout, Howard eventually decided to call a halt to the flogging, but the respite was to be short-lived, as a crewman was sent to fetch gunpowder from down below, which Howard ordered to be rubbed into Baku's wounds, forcing the brave warrior to scream in sheer agony. Now satisfied, Howard ordered the flogging to resume, and once he had finally got his five hundred lashes, he gestured for Baku's limp, lifeless body to be unceremoniously thrown overboard.

'More food for the sharks,' a sniggering crewman was heard to say.

Kwento was stunned, but could only look on as all the slaves, both men and women, were led back down into the hold with their heads lowered, appearing totally exhausted and dejected. Despite feeling completely demoralised himself, Kwento did not miss his chance to discreetly hand the long, rusty nail to Akin as he moved to take up his position next to the captain, and with a knowing nod from Baku's hand-picked successor, insurrection was back on the table.

Akin knew that if the rebellion was to succeed, he would have to act fast, while there was still anger in the faces of the slaves. He was banking on the fact that Baku had become very popular among the group, and would no doubt be regarded as a black hero, a true warrior and, most importantly of all, a martyr following his heroic sacrifice. Being one of the first to have his manacles replaced, Akin waited patiently for the crewmen to finish chaining up the others, all the while staring down at the long, rusty nail in his hand.

The nail is the key, he thought. The key to salvation. The key to freedom. The key to emancipation.

When the opportunity to speak arrived, he explained his position in a low, calm voice.

'We will wait until nightfall, and then, once released, we must take the ship immediately,' he said, 'and give no quarter to captain or crew. We must kill all the white men. Agreed?'

The slaves all quietly nodded their assent and waited patiently for nightfall to come, as Akin began releasing only the most able-bodied; those who he was confident would not simply get in the way. He felt angry and belligerent, his heart pumping with adrenaline as he began to taste revenge for the death of Baku, who had not just been a fellow tribesman, but also a close friend. He was not as measured or cerebral as Baku in his approach to battle, preferring to launch wild, berserker-style attacks, which would result in him leading the slaves with his heart rather than his head. His rage was blinding him to the reality of the situation, not to mention steering him off the course that Baku had so carefully plotted for them.

Free of their shackles, the slaves crept around searching for anything that they could use as a weapon, before making their way up to the next level, the crews' sleeping berth, where they found Sam Pretty, Riley, Baxter and Smith all tucked up in their hammocks.

His head still bandaged, Pretty was chosen as their first victim, only for Akin to change his mind and order three of the men to gag and throttle Riley, Baxter and Smith first. He then gestured for them to kill the boatswain while he slept, but as the slave leaned over the slumbering body, Pretty awoke with a start and plunged his knife deep into the bare chest of his would-be assailant, killing him instantly. This forced Akin to break ranks and charge forward, dagger in hand, towards the bigger, stronger man, who in his depleted state was slow to react to the younger, faster and more experienced warrior. They began to wrestle, each holding the other firmly by the throat with one hand whilst parrying knives with the other, followed by lots of shouting and cursing, jabbing and slashing, as the air quickly filled with the heavy odour of sweat and fresh blood. The noise woke Thomas Wales and Dara, and the first mate sprung quickly from his bunk and got dressed, grabbing his pistol and cutlass as he headed for the door. Dara seized him by the arm, begging him not to get involved, but he curtly dismissed her pleas, explaining that though he did not like his captain, it was his duty to protect him.

Kwento stayed hidden in the shadows, observing the scene from a safe distance, though close enough to be shocked to his core by the level of brutality on display, making him feel sick to his stomach. He had been under no illusions about what it would take to seize control of the ship, but still he was stunned by what transpired before him, as suddenly everything fell silent, and Sam Pretty fell back dead into his beige hammock, which began to darken as it became soaked with the boatswain's blood. The bloodletting had started, and there was no turning back.

From there, Akin led the rebels on to the upper deck, where a mass brawl quickly broke out, but he had only one objective in mind: to get to Captain Howard's quarters as quickly as possible. There was, however, one obstacle standing in his way as he climbed the six broad wooden steps up to the quarter deck, as Thomas Wales stood before him, armed with a pistol in one hand and a blade in the other, determined to protect his captain.

As Akin approached, Wales levelled his pistol and pulled the trigger, but after holding his breath and waiting for the impact from the lead ball, the young warrior realised that the pistol had misfired. Sensing an opportunity, he lunged forward and, daggers drawn, a brief struggle ensued, which ended with Wales hitting the deck hard, clutching at his throat. His wife's premonition had come to bear, as the first mate lay dead on the quarter deck, with Dara screaming at the top of her voice as she dashed across and threw her body down over his, her dreams of freedom now dead.

His path clear, Akin entered the captain's quarters, where he was once again confronted by a pistol aimed squarely at his chest. Howard cocked the weapon, but just as he was about to squeeze the trigger, Kwento appeared and grabbed a half-filled tankard of ale that he then threw in Howard's face, temporarily blinding him. As a result, the bullet narrowly missed its target, becoming lodged in the door behind him, allowing Akin to grab the pistol and apprehend the captain, before tying him to his own chair.

Of the fifty crewmen, only nineteen survived, including the captain and the surgeon.

'This ship is now under my control, Captain,' Akin declared.

'Yes, it would appear so,' Howard mumbled. 'Are any of my crew still alive?'

'Thomas Wales and Sam Pretty are both dead, but there are a few men still alive, despite my orders to kill them all. It would appear that those who have been kind to the slaves were spared, which doesn't say much for your chances, Captain.'

'Was Thomas Wales not kind to you? Did he not take one of the black whores for his woman.'

'Thomas Wales was one I didn't have a problem with him, but he chose to die protecting you. If he hadn't barred my way to you, he would still be alive this day.'

'What you have done here cannot be undone,' Howard shook his head. 'May God have mercy on your soul.'

'It's not forgiveness I'm looking for, Captain. Just your ship.'

'Well, now you have it. The question is, what do you intend to do with it, may I ask?'

'We are going back.'

'What do you mean "back?" Back where? We're adrift in the middle of the ocean, man.'

'I'm taking this vessel back to Africa, to undo what you have done.'

'You're a bloody fool if you think you can pull this one off. You'll never make it. You do realise that, don't you?'

'We are going back, Captain. That's all there is to it.'

'Think about it, man. You've killed nearly all my crew, including my first officer and boatswain, so who is going to navigate? Who is going to set the sails, and what about our supplies?'

'Supplies?'

'Yes, supplies. We have just about enough food and fresh water to get to the Americas, but if you turn back now, we will certainly be dead before reaching Africa.'

'So, what would you have me do, Captain?'

'You must hand control of the ship back to me. Then, maybe, with what little crew I have left, we might just make it to America. It's the only way.

Akin had to admit that Howard did have a valid point. In his thirst for revenge, he had not factored all this into his plan. In fact, he had completely overlooked it. Neither he nor any of the other slaves possessed even basic knowledge of seamanship, having never piloted anything bigger than longboat or gone further than along the banks of the River Niger. They had no hope of manoeuvring a huge, heavy vessel through deep, open waters, leaving him with no choice but to confront the futility of attempting to sail back to Africa.

'Truth be told, I'm not confident that we could even make it to America at this point,' Howard said. 'We were still five weeks away from New Orleans when you launched your bloody coup, and we've drifted way off course since then.'

Akin might have proved himself as a leader and warrior, but

the situation had changed such that he now needed to become a diplomat. Thus, he reluctantly untied Captain Howard before pulling up a chair and sitting down opposite him, rubbing his chin in deep thought.

'Why are you freeing him?' Kwento asked, in a low voice. 'What's going on?'

'I'm trying to make things right, little warrior,' Akin forced a smile, despite his obvious uncertainty.

'But we've won – we've won!' Kwento continued, getting increasingly angry and confused.

'No, little warrior,' Akin said sadly, gently stroking the boy's head.

'I don't understand,' Kwento's eyes filled with tears. 'Why would you even think of getting into bed with this man after everything that's happened, especially now that the ship is under our control?'

He was too young to realise that the thought of handing back power to Captain Howard was just as horrifying to Akin as it was to him, but that given the circumstances, there was little other choice. Akin did not believe all was lost, though. His hope was that if he could cut a deal to save the captain's life in exchange for a full pardon and freedom for all the slaves once they reach the Americas, even though it meant breaking Baku's golden rule to never trust the white man or his promises.

'A promise is only a comfort to a fool,' as Baku would often say.

Of course, Howard agreed to Akin's terms, knowing full well that with nothing written down on paper, it would simply be a matter of reneging on the deal once they reached New Orleans. Not only did he have no intention of honouring a single part of their agreement, he was actively plotting his revenge, and upon reaching America, he promptly had Akin stripped naked and left to hang from the jib of the Douglas, as an example to anyone else who might want to follow his lead. Kwento, Dara and the rest of the slaves were all sold on the quayside for two hundred dollars each, and then dispatched to various plantations across the country's deep south. Kwento found himself on a cotton farm in Savanna, Georgia, where he joined a hundred others in enduring back-breaking labour, working sixteen-hour days while regularly suffering the master's whip. He would be moved around numerous plantations over the course of the following six years, until he was eventually settled in Virginia.

Meanwhile, Howard's remaining crew decided to mutiny and jump ship in New Orleans, as Dr Green had predicted, leaving him with no choice other than to replace them with American sailors before setting sail back to England, where, twelve months later, Captain John 'Flogger' Howard died of a heart attack at his home in Hampshire. As for the Douglas, she was renamed the Devon, as she continued her service until she was finally decommissioned in 1823.

PART TWO

BECOMING BARTHOLD

WATER STREET, LIVERPOOL TOWN CENTRE, 1827

It was eleven o'clock on a dull, wet Wednesday morning, and the wealthy cotton merchant Colin Strome was attending a slave auction outside the old coffee house on Water Street. Before him stood three negro males brought in from the Coburg Dock, all bound together with ropes and chains connecting their iron neck collars. The two older ones had come direct from the Calabar, the branded initials still fresh on their cheeks, while the youngest, shipped over from America, looked unspoilt. Strome had no real interest in slavery, but curiosity had compelled him to stop and watch as the auctioneer mounted his soapbox and started playing to the small crowd that was gathered in the drizzling rain.

It didn't take long for the two branded slaves to sell for the sum of fifteen guineas each, but the younger one, who presented as a mute, did not receive a single bid.

'Sir,' the auctioneer called out to Strome, as the crowd began to lose interest and disperse, 'look at this fine young specimen. He is sober and humane, with a most pleasant disposition.'

Strome looked back at the small, robust man, whose round, ruddy face ended in a large ginger beard.

'He's muscular,' the auctioneer continued, waving his long bamboo cane, which he occasionally used to prod at the young slave, 'and even has all his own teeth, see? He would make a wonderful page boy. Here, come and take a look for yourself.'

'No, thank you,' Strome politely declined.

'For you, a bargain price of just twelve guineas. What say you, sir?'

'No, thank you.'

'You drive a hard bargain, sir… Nine guineas, and that's my final offer.'

'I'm really not that interested,' Strome began to turn away, 'but thank you all the same.'

Clearly agitated, the auctioneer removed his black top hat and scratched at his bald head.

'OK, I'll tell you what I'm going to do,' he said, 'and this really is my final offer. Seven guineas – I'm practically giving him away. What say you, sir?'

'No, thank you,' Strome said firmly.

'Well, that is most unfortunate.'

'And why is that?'

'If I can't sell him, I'll have to cut his throat

'Good God, man,' Strome exclaimed in horror, you can't be serious? He's a human being.'

'Nevertheless, if I can't sell him, he's no use to me.'

'Right, give him to me,' Strome sighed. 'I will take him.'

He extended his hand towards the auctioneer, as for the first time in his life, he became the owner of a slave. He then flagged down a hackney carriage, loaded the boy into it and was on his way home.

The cab pulled up sharply at the kerb of 19 Folly Fields, Oxford Street, and Strome led the slave down into the front lightwell of his house and rapped on the door to the tradesmen's entrance, which was slowly opened by Polly, the scullery maid, who stood rigid with fright at the sight of the exotic black figure standing before her. Inside, the cook, Mrs Alsop, and the butler, Mr Bailey, greeted the newest addition to the staff with their arms folded tightly in front of them, with looks of unrestrained indignation painted brightly on their faces.

'Right, gather around everyone,' Strome ordered. 'This is our new house boy, Barthold.'

'Barthold!' Mrs Alsop cried.

'That is correct,' Strome replied matter-of-factly.

'But – that's your name, sir.'

'Indeed, but you see, Mrs Alsop, the poor wretch has no name of his own.'

'Why hasn't he got his own name, sir?' Polly piped up.

'Oh, shut up, Polly!' Mrs Alsop hissed.

'He has no name because he's a mute,' Strome answered.

'Begging your pardon, sir, but why would you buy a mute with no name?'

'My dear fellow,' Strome laughed, 'I got him for a song, he was that cheap.'

'Search the Holly book,' Mrs Alsop tutted, putting her hands on her hips. 'Do you mean to say that you actually paid for this heathen, sir?'

'If you'd be so kind as to feed the poor wretch,' Strome dodged the question. 'Oh, and Mr Bailey?'

'Sir?'

'Once Barthold is fed, kindly clean him up and dress him in some of Henry's old clothes. I think they should fit nicely.'

An audible gasp filled the air, and then the kitchen fell silent as the staff exchanged furtive glances with fear in their eyes. Nobody had so much as entered Henry's bedroom in the preceding two years; not since Mrs Strome had turned it into a shrine to her deceased son, complete with full military dress remaining laid out neatly on his bed. She could never accept Henry's death, and was often heard talking about him as though he were still alive. The loss had also changed her personality, making her quick to anger, and causing long mood swings that kept the staff on edge due to their growing unpredictability.

'But, sir,' Bailey finally spoke up, having been nudged by Mrs Alsop, 'the mistress has given us strict instructions that no one is to enter master Henry's bedroom under any circumstances.'

'Mr Bailey, may I remind you that I am in charge here,' Strome said, 'not Mrs Strome. Now, get it done. Oh, and by the way, the slave doesn't understand English.'

'Doesn't understand the King's English!' Mrs Alsop exclaimed, raising her eyes up to the heavens. 'Well, begging your pardon, sir, but how on earth are we to communicate with it, then?'

'Make do and mend, Mrs Alsop,' Strome smiled wryly. 'Make do and mend. That reminds me, Mr Bailey?'

'Sir?'

'I'm charging you with providing his Christian education. Give him a copy of the New Testament and teach him the scriptures, as well as our own house protocols, of course.'

'Yes, Mr Strome.'

Unhappy though he obviously was with the situation, Bailey knew that he had no choice other than to obey his master's wishes, so he turned to Kwento, patted him on the shoulder and, with a thin smile, took his leave of the kitchen. As for Kwento, his nostrils had been filling with the warm, sweet smell of freshly-baked bread, and this was making him very hungry. He could also feel the heat radiating from the large, old black stove, which had three fat copper saucepans bubbling away on top of it, and decided to quietly position himself as close to it as possible. His first impressions of his new surroundings were quite positive, and he was pleased to have arrived in England. The British crew aboard the Merry had treated him well on the voyage from America to Liverpool, allowing him feel like a real person for the first time since his initial capture back in Africa. He had shared their food rations and slept in the same berth, and hoped that things would similar here.

Plus, I've lived under far worse conditions than this, he thought.

Mrs Alsop placed a large black kettle on the stove, and then set three cups and saucers around the table with a plate of macaroons in the middle. Mr Bailey and Polly each took a seat, as they waited for Mrs Alsop to play mother and pour the tea.

'I just don't know what to say, Mr Bailey,' Mrs Alsop shook her head, 'I really don't. The master has gone and lost all his marbles. I mean, what was he thinking, bringing that African into this house?'

'It's his house, Mrs Alsop,' Bailey shrugged. 'He can do as he pleases.'

'Oh, so you think it's perfectly alright, do you?'

'No, not at all. I feel exactly as you do. I'm simply saying, what choice do we have in the matter?'

'What choice indeed,' Mrs Alsop complained bitterly. 'Mark my words, this African will disrupt the harmony and smooth running of this household. A good, decent house, thrown into disrepute on a silly whim.'

'Again, I agree wholeheartedly, Mrs Alsop.'

'Well, I don't agree,' Polly chirped. 'I think he could brighten up this dingy old place. God knows, it could do with some livening.'

'If I want your opinion, missy, I'll ask for it,' Mrs Alsop snapped. 'And don't blaspheme at this table, thank you very much!'

'I was only saying, Mrs Alsop–'

'Oh, shut up and pass my delicious homemade macaroons to Mr Bailey, if you please,' Mrs Alsop cut the younger woman off.

'Ah, your macaroons are simply to die for, Mrs Alsop,' Bailey smiled.

'Why, thank you, Mr Bailey,' Mrs Alsop nodded approvingly.

'Yes, that's why they're called "Mrs Alsop's delicious homemade macaroons,"' Polly said, snatching one up and stuffing it unceremoniously into her mouth.'

'Where are your manners, girl?' Mrs Alsop asked incredulously. 'You eat like a dockworker.'

'Oh, she just likes her food is all, Mrs Alsop,' Bailey said.

'Yes, I can see that,' Mrs Alsop smirked, 'judging by the size of her hips.'

'That's not fair, Mrs Alsop,' Polly protested. 'I might not be as skinny as Miss Sarah, but I'm not fat!'

'How dare you talk about Miss Sarah like that,' Mrs Alsop flared. 'She's not skinny, she's slim and elegant. And yes, you are fat, you big, great lump!'

'Mr Bailey, please, I'm not fat, am I?' Polly sobbed.

'Now, now, Polly,' Mr Bailey said, 'don't you go getting yourself all upset. I'm sure Mrs Alsop meant nothing by it. Did you, Mrs Alsop?'

'Well–'

'There, you see, no harm done. Now, dry your eyes and have another macaroon.'

'Do you think that's wise, Mr Bailey?' Mrs Alsop said under her breath.

'Oh, please, Mrs Alsop,' Polly stuck out her bottom lip.

'Ahem,' Mrs Alsop coughed, rising from the table. 'Anyway, you heard what the master said, Mr Bailey. Best fetch some clothes whilst I feed the darky. Oh, and Polly?'

'Yes, Mrs Alsop?'

'Stay well clear of this black rogue, do you hear me?'

'Yes, Mrs Alsop… Mrs Alsop?'

'Yes, Polly?'

'What do they eat?'

'What does who eat?'

'Africans.'

'Search the Holly book! How the hell should I know?'

'I only mean, if he can't speak, how do we find out what he eats? What if he doesn't like our food?'

'Shut up, Polly! I'll give him a nice bowl of my thick, rich scouse, and if he doesn't like it, he can bloody well starve!'

With that, Bailey took his leave, while Mrs Alsop marched over to the black stove and began stirring the large brass pot with a long-handled wooden spoon.

'Nobody can resist your thick, rich scouse, Mrs Alsop,' Polly grinned. 'Mrs Alsop?'

'Yes, Polly?'

'Why can't he speak?'

'What do you mean?'

'The master says he's mute, which means he can't speak. I was just wondering why.'

'How the hell should I know?'

'I thought you knew everything about everything, Mrs Alsop.'

'Is this an attempt at sarcasm, young miss?'

'No, no, Mrs Alsop, I would never. It's just that you know a lot is all.

Mrs Alsop scooped out some of the thick, rich scouse from the bubbling brass pot, before taking a sip from the long-handled wooden spoon and smacking her lips. She then placed the lid back onto the pot, walked back over to the dining table and sat down.

'Oi, Barthold, or whatever your bloody name is,' she said. 'Come here and put your arse to anchor.'

Kwento stood and stared at Mrs Alsop, having no intention of moving from the warmth of the large black stove.

'They've probably cut his tongue clean out of his head,' Mrs Alsop concluded.

'I beg your pardon, Mrs Alsop!' Polly gasped.

'You know what these Africans are like, they'll have cut it out. It'll be some silly tribal thing is all.'

'Dear God, how awful!'

'Don't blaspheme, Polly! Why is he just standing there? Is he deaf as well as dumb?'

'I think it's the stove he likes, Mrs Alsop. He hasn't moved from it since he came in. Maybe he's cold.'

'Cold indeed,' Mrs Alsop scoffed. 'He's just bone-bloody-idle more like. Here, take a seat at the table.'

'It's very hot in Africa.'

'Been there yourself, have you?'

'No, but my father served in Africa he did, and he said it was as hot as hell over there.'

'Language please, Polly.'

'It's true, Mrs Alsop. Father used to call them fuzzy wuzzies.'

'Barthold!' Mrs Alsop roared. 'Will you get over here!'

Determined not move away from the hot black stove, Kwento continued to stand and stare in silent insolence.

Why can't she just leave me alone? he thought. It's so cold and damp down here.

It was already obvious that this Mrs Alsop had no interest in him or his culture, and he began to wonder if the British were no different than the Americans, and would also see him as nothing more than a savage.

'Oh, my giddy aunt,' Alsop threw up her hands in exasperation. 'I give up. Polly, you try getting through to him.'

'Come on, Barthold,' Polly said gently, patting an empty chair. 'It's time to eat.'

Something in the younger woman's manner appealed to Kwento, and after a moment's deliberation, he slowly eased himself away from the warmth of the stove and took a seat at the large, heavy wooden table.

'Mrs Alsop?'

'Yes, Polly?'

'Why is Barthold wearing a metal collar?'

'Isn't it obvious?'

'Not to me.'

'That's because you're a silly child, Polly. It's to stop him from running away.'

'But… how can a metal neck collar stop him from running away?'

'Search the Holly book! You pass a chain through the collar and fix the chain to the wall. Then, he can't run away. Understand?'

'How cruel!'

'Watch your mouth, young lady.'

Mrs Alsop fetched a lump of dried bread and placed it down next to the white china bowl that sat untouched in front of Kwento.

'Here,' she said, 'get that down you, and you won't know your queen from Aunt.'

Kwento ignored the spoon and, taking the bowl in both hands, proceeded to swallow its contents whole in a matter of seconds. He then let out an enormous belch, right as an attractive, well-dressed young lady was entering the kitchen.

'See, nobody can resist your rich, thick scouse, Mrs Alsop,' Polly giggled.

'Indeed,' Mrs Alsop shook her head at Kwento's lack of etiquette, before leaping to her feet and curtseying at the sight of the newcomer. 'Oh, Miss Sarah, what brings you down here?'

'I've come to see Daddy's new house boy,' Miss Sarah said, 'but look at him, he's all skin and bones!'

'Not for long, Miss Sarah,' Polly said, indicating the empty bowl. 'Look, he's wolfed the bleeding lot.'

'Language, Polly,' Mrs Alsop rolled her ey's.

'But you always say "bloody," Mrs Alsop.'

'Haven't you got work to be doing?'

'Yes, Mrs Alsop.'

'Well then, jump to it, girl. Them beds won't make themselves, you know.'

'Yes, Mrs Alsop.'

As Polly turned to leave the kitchen, Mr Bailey returned wearing a huge grin on his face, with some of Henry's old clothes folded over his arm.

'Here you are, my young sambo,' he beamed, 'these should fit nicely.'

'Very well,' Mrs Alsop sighed, 'but take the black devil to the scullery and clean him up first.'

'Wait a minute,' Miss Sarah said, her voice full of concern, 'they're Henry's clothes, aren't they?'

'That is correct, Miss. Sarah,' Bailey nodded.

'What are you doing with them? No one is allowed in Henry's room.'

'Mr Bailey is only following your father's orders, Miss Sarah,' Mrs Alsop explained.

'Oh, is he?' Miss Sarah shrieked. 'Well, we will see about that!'

As the young lady of the house stormed off to confront her father upstairs in the morning room, Bailey led his charge into the scullery and began filling a small bathtub with kettles of hot water while Kwento undressed.

'Right, me lad-o, in you go,' Bailey gestured towards the water.

Kwento stood frozen and covering his modesty, much to the butler's annoyance.

'Come on, lad, you've nothing I haven't seen before.'

Kwento reluctantly lowered his arms and stepped into the tub, and Bailey could not help but stare at the long scars that ran across his back. He was no stranger to the slave trade himself, having worked as a shipping clerk for the Gregson slaving syndicate back in 1789. They had owned a ship called the Brookes, which held up to four hundred and fifty slaves all told. The vessel was reported to have ferried some fifty-eight thousand African slaves to the West Indies before being retired in 1804, and the Gregson syndicate were also insurers of Captain Luke Collingwood's ship the Zong, which due to Collingwood's poor navigational skills, got lost on a voyage to Jamaica in 1781. This resulted in a shortage of drinking water, prompting Collingwood to throw more than one hundred slaves overboard to save on supplies, before later demanding that Gregson cover losses over livestock, in a claim that was eventually rejected as fraudulent. Because of the scandal that followed, Bailey decided to sever all ties with the Gregson company and enter into service.

'Bloody hell, matey,' Bailey grimaced, 'you've been in the wars, haven't you?'

'What's going on back there?' Mrs Alsop called through from the kitchen.

'Nothing for you to worry about, Mrs Alsop,' Bailey answered. 'The black heathen's got whip marks all across his back is all.'

'Um, well, if he's been beaten, he probably deserved it. You need to get him dressed before the master comes down… Now, where is Polly. She'll be the death of me that girl.'

Mrs Alsop found Polly standing outside the morning room, with her ear pressed up hard against the doors.

'Search the Holly book!' she hissed. 'What are you doing, child? Get away from there right now!'

'Miss Sarah and Mr and Mrs Strome are having the most terribly row, Mrs Alsop,' Polly said.

'Now, you listen to me, young madam. You're to get yourself down to the kitchen and start peeling them spuds, before I take the strap to you. Go on!'

'Yes, Mrs Alsop,' Polly said, walking away quickly.

Once she was sure that Polly had gone, Mrs Alsop turned and put her eye up against the gap in the doors. Inside, the master's wife Agnes was sitting on the sofa, with daughter Sarah alongside her.

They were both staring at Mr Strome, who was standing at the fireplace dressed in a three-quarter-length black coat over a starched white shirt, black cravat and a beige waistcoat, looking down at the gold fob watch in his hand.

'How could you be so cruel?' Mrs Strome asked, her voice breaking.

'I'm sorry, darling,' Mr Strome said, wearing a puzzled look on his face.

'First, you bring a blackamoor into our home, and then you decide to give him our family name!'

'My dear, he was going so cheap, I simply had to take him. I really don't see what all the fuss is about.'

Strome decided not to tell his wife and daughter the real reason why he bought the slave, as he thought the truth might be far too distressing for them.

'You've dressed him in Henry's clothes! How could you? How could you?'

Mrs Strome took out a handkerchief from under her sleeve, and pinched her nose as she began to weep.

'Yes, Daddy, how could you?' Miss Sarah put in. 'And now look what you've done to poor Mummy.'

'Oh, calm yourselves please,' Strome looked up from his watch. 'On the matter of the family name, the boy is a mute, he has no name of his own, so I gave him one of mine. I see no wrong in that, and as for Henry's clothes, Henry has been dead two years now, my dear.'

'Yes, murdered by savages the Ashanti,' Mrs Strome spat. 'Savages like that one downstairs. I will not tolerate his presence under my roof, do you hear?'

'Come on now, darling, you can't blame Henry's death on poor

Barthold,' Strome said. 'We don't even know what tribe he's from.'

'Now it's poor Barthold!' Mrs Strome cried. 'They're all savages, Colin. Have you forgot what they did to Henry – to your son? He was sent to Nsamankow to protect the governor, Sir Charles McCarthy. Five hundred British troops against ten thousand warriors. They never stood a chance. That's why I hate all Africans!'

The atmosphere was sombre and strained, but Strome was determined to lift the mood by injecting his own strange brand of humour.

'You liked Ira Aldridge, my dear,' he said. 'You thought his portrayal of Othello was fantastic.'

'That's different,' Mrs Strome snarled. 'He's an actor.'

'He's also a negro, darling.'

'Stop trying to confuse me, Colin! Besides, he's much better than that drunken sot who you like.'

Pleased that he had successfully diverted his wife's attention away from Barthold for the moment, Strome decided to take a seat.

'If you're referring to Mr George Cooke,' he said, 'then I must say, he was one of the finest actors ever to tread the boards.'

'"Finest actors" – ha! The last time he played in Liverpool, he was an absolute disgrace.

'What do you mean by that?'

'Colin, the man arrived on stage as drunk as a lord, and when he was rightly booed by the audience, he went into a demented rage, ranting about how he had not come here to be insulted by a set of wretches, and charging that every brick in our "infernal town" is "cemented with an African's blood!"'

'Now, be fair, darling, he was treated very badly by the audience. It was just a simple retort on his part, that's all.'

'Stop trying to distract me! The matter at hand is the African. He can't possibly be trusted. They beheaded McCarthy, and then ate his heart and used his skull as a drinking bowl.'

'You merely lack a full understanding of the Ashanti, my dear. What they did may seem horrid to us, but to them, it was a ritual honouring of a great warrior.'

'Why did Henry have to go to that godforsaken place anyway?'

Mrs Strome became very distressed again, and had to be comforted by her daughter as she began to weep.

'He was sent there because we formed an alliance with the Fanti,' Strome said matter-of-factly. 'Thus, it was our duty to protect them from the Ashanti.'

He then watched as his wife rose from her sofa then walked over to the large bay window, with its view of Abercromby Park.

'I don't care who made alliances with whom,' she said quietly. 'I just want him gone. He's an animal.'

'I disagree, Mummy,' Miss Sarah spoke up. 'I think he's quite cute, in a funny sort of way.'

'There, you see,' Strome cheered. 'Even Sarah sees the benefit in having Barthold around.'

'Yes, can we keep him please, Mummy?' Miss Sarah pleaded. 'Jane's father has a blackamoor. It's all the fashion these days.'

'He's not a blackamoor, Sarah,' Strome laughed. 'He's an African.'

'Fashion indeed!' Mrs Strome rolled her eyes. 'The brute has already beguiled this family with his juju black magic. I hope you're both very pleased with yourselves.'

'Well, that's it settled, then,' Strome said. 'I should add, I've instructed Bailey to teach Barthold our Christian ways. That should take the beast out of him, eh?'

'Very well,' Mrs Strome blew out her cheeks, as Miss Sarah clasped her hands together in excitement, 'but know this. One wrong move from that black brute, and he's out. Do you both understand?'

'Anyone for a cup of tea?' Strome asked.

'Oh, yes please, Daddy,' Miss Sarah jumped up and down on the spot, 'with jam and scones.'

Strome cranked the brass dial next to the fireplace, signalling to the staff downstairs that their services were needed, and causing Mrs Alsop to pull herself away from the door and run back to the kitchen as fast as her legs would carry her.

'Don't he look a picture, eh?' Bailey said, presenting a freshly bathed and dressed Kwento.

'Oh, yes,' Polly agreed. 'You look very smart, Barthold – very smart indeed. Now, I'll have to get those potatoes peeled, otherwise Mrs Alsop said she will beat me.'

'Surely not,' Bailey laughed. 'I think she was only playing with you.'

'Well, playing or not, I'd better get on with it.'

'Of course, don't let me keep you… Oh, but Polly?'

'Yes, Mr Bailey?'

'It's just that I have two tickets for the theatre tomorrow night, and I was wondering if you would like to accompany me?'

'Oh, Mr Bailey, I–'

'Please, call me Edward.'

'I'm sorry, Edward, but I'm very busy tomorrow night.'

'I see,' Bailey ran a hand through his receding brown hair. 'It's because of my age, isn't it?'

'Pardon?'

'You think I'm too old for you, don't you?'

'Not at all, Mr Bailey – I mean, Edward.'

Polly was being honest when she said it had nothing to do with his age. The truth was that she would never accept such an offer from him because she was fully aware of his shameful past employment, though she would refrain from revealing this knowledge so long as he continued to treat her with respect.

'It's alright, Polly, I understand,' he said dejectedly. 'I should never have asked. I feel so stupid now.'

'I really didn't mean to offend you, Edward.'

'It's quite alright. You know what they say, there's no fool like an old fool.'

Polly had probably never been so happy to see Mrs Alsop's face, as the cook came racing into the kitchen all flustered, and frantically set about making a pot of tea with scones.

'Ah, Mrs Alsop,' she said, indicating Kwento's new outfit. 'What do you think of our Barthold, then? He looks a new man, wouldn't you agree?'

'Well, I must admit, it's quite the transformation,' Mrs Alsop nodded approvingly. 'Doesn't he look like the cat that's got the cream. You've done a marvellous job on him, Mr Bailey. I mean, he almost looks human.'

'Why, thank you, Mrs Alsop,' Bailey took a bow.

'Mind you, we'll have to keep an eye on him. He's got that in the night look about him.'

'Whatever do you mean, Mrs Alsop?'

'Let's just say that until he's fully house trained, we should consider him a potential runner.'

'Surely not, Mrs Alsop. I mean, even if he did try to flee, he wouldn't be hard to find now, would he?'

'Is that so? And just how would you find him if he did flee, Chief Inspector Bailey?'

Bailey began to pace back and forth in mock concentration,

mimicking a detective with his thumbs neatly tucked under his smart black jacket lapels.

'First, I would proceed to the Toxteth Park area,' he said with a glint in his eye, 'or Little Africa, as it is more commonly known.'

'Little Africa!' Mrs Alsop exclaimed, her horror evident.

'Why, yes. Everyone knows that Stanhope Street and Gore Street are where the runaway slaves go when they flee their masters.'

'Nevertheless, Mr Bailey, the master's paid real money for this wretch, and we need to protect his investment.'

'What do you suggest?'

'You're the one who's been put in charge of him. You tell me.'

'True, but then I lack your – how should I put it? – worldly experience in these matters, Mrs Alsop.'

'Oh, you've a silver tongue in your head, Mr Bailey. I suggest we make use of his brass neck collar.'

'Meaning?'

'Meaning you chain him up, and I'd do it right now if I were you.'

'But where shall I affix him?'

'Search the Holly book! Do I have to think of everything? Make up a cot and stick him in the scullery.'

'Of course, Mrs Alsop.'

'And make sure the black rogue is chained up good and proper,' she added. 'We don't want him wandering around the house in the middle of the night now, do we?'

'Certainly not, Mrs Alsop. That just wouldn't do at all.'

Later that day, Bailey went and quietly tapped on the large, brown four-panelled doors of the morning room, before turning the ornate brass handles and entering. Inside, Strome was sitting at his bureau, penning a letter.

'May I have a word, sir?' Bailey asked cautiously.

'Certainly,' Strome looked up from his writing. 'What is it?'

'Well, sir, Mrs Alsop and myself were thinking it would be prudent to secure the slave during the hours of darkness, sir.'

'Secure the slave, you say?'

'Yes, sir.'

'And why would I want to do that?'

'To stop him fleeing, sir.'

'Fleeing?'

'That's correct, sir. Just a precaution until he's fully house trained, of course, sir.'

'Do you really think it necessary, Mr Bailey?'

'Oh, absolutely, sir.'

'Very well, Mr Bailey. I will accept your recommendation – for now.'

'Thank you, sir.'

'Is there anything else?'

'Um, just one more thing, sir.'

'Yes, Bailey?'

'You may also wish to consider having the slave branded, sir.'

'Branded! What in heaven's name for?'

'If he should break his bonds, it would be easier to track him down, sir. You could have your initials stamped on his shoulder blades or on his chest. You could even have them stamped on his forehead, if you so wish. I know a blacksmith on the Dock Road who would be able to do it, sir.'

'No, out of the question,' Strome frowned. 'You seem to have a great knowledge of matters relating to slavery, Mr Bailey. Where did you acquire it?'

Is the master on to me? Bailey wondered aghast, as his mouth suddenly became dry. Has the past finally caught up with me, or is it just my conscience playing tricks? Perhaps the ghosts of all those poor, wretched slaves I helped send to the Americas and West Indies have tracked me down at last.

Liverpool was filled with people who had benefited from slavery, from sail makers, rope makers and gunsmiths, to iron mongers, coopers, riggers and carpenters. The Gregson Slaving Syndicate for whom Bailey had worked were directly responsible for sending fifty-eight thousand African slaves to the new world, in addition to the staggering one million-plus that were sent to Brazil, the Caribbean and the Americas by the group of thirty-seven town councillors and local merchants.

'Oh, you know how it is, sir,' Bailey tugged at his collar. 'You just pick things up is all. Anyway, as I was saying, old Lenny the blacksmith has done it many times before. He brands all the slaves that come off the brigantines.'

Strome sprung up from his leather easy chair and strode right up close to his butler.

'Now, look here,' he said, looking more cross than Bailey had ever seen him before, 'I'll not have Barthold branded, like some bull or heifer. The whole idea is ungodly, and I'll hear no more of it. Do you understand me?'

'Yes, sir,' Bailey lowered his head. 'Sorry, sir.'

Returning to the kitchen, Bailey joined Mrs Alsop and Polly at the large oak dining table, as Barthold sat quietly on his cot in the scullery, chained to the wall. After taking a mouthful from the steaming bowl that had been left out for him, the butler then dabbed the corners of his mouth with a crisp white napkin before speaking.

'Well, I must say, Mrs Alsop, that rabbit stew was absolutely delicious,' he said effusively. 'First class – first class.'

'Why, thank you, Mr Bailey,' Mrs Alsop blushed. 'And how is yours, Polly?'

'It's fine, thanks.'

'Only fine?'

'I don't really like rabbit.'

'How can you not like rabbit?'

The cook folded her arms under her breasts and lifted them slightly, something she only did when very annoyed.

'Don't you go getting yourself all upset, Mrs Alsop,' Bailey said, attempting to ease the tension before it could develop further. 'There's no accounting for personal tastes, and I'm sure Polly wasn't making a comment on your cooking ability, were you, Polly?'

'Not at all,' Polly shook her head.

'So, what sort of things do you like?' Mrs Alsop asked the young housekeeper.

'Faggots,' Polly squeaked.

'I beg your pardon!'

'If you served faggots, I'd scoff the lot straight down.'

'You know, you've a real foul mouth on you for a young lass,' Mrs Alsop shook her head. '"Scoff it down," what sort of talk is that?'

'Now, now, Mrs Alsop,' Bailey once again felt the need to intervene, 'I'm sure the girl meant nothing by it.'

'I should hope not,' Mrs Alsop said, staring a hole through Polly.

'What's for pudding, Mrs Alsop?' Polly whispered.

'What's for pudding! You've got some brass neck on you, young lady.'

'Oh, but Mrs Alsop, I thought it was Barthold who had the brass neck?'

'Don't you be getting all cocky with me, young madam.'

'Come on, please tell us what's for pudding, Mrs. Alsop. You know how much we love your puddings.

'Yes,' Bailey joined in, 'please tell us, Mrs Alsop.

'Well, if you must know, it's jam roly-poly.'

'Ah,' Bailey rubbed his hands together, 'my favourite. With lots of thick, rich custard, I hope?'

'But of course, Mr Bailey. Come give me a hand, Polly.'

Before making the custard, Mrs Alsop instructed Polly to take a hot bowl of rabbit stew to Barthold, having realised that she'd forgot all about him.

'Poor, poor Barthold,' Polly said, handing him the bowl and a spoon, and then pulling up a chair alongside his cot. 'Where have you been? Where do you come from? Please tell me of your world… Oh, if only you could speak. Your eyes tell me that you've seen far more, and know far more, than we ever could.'

Polly hadn't noticed that Bailey had positioned himself in the doorway of the scullery, as he intended to follow up on his suspicion that she was attracted to the young slave.

'You like him, don't you?' he asked, flashing a sardonic grin.

'This treatment is inhumane,' she said. 'To chain someone to a wall is ghastly, Mr Bailey. It goes against the will of God.'

'You didn't answer my question.'

'I just feel sorry for him is all,' she said, turning to avoid his gaze.

'Pudding's out!' Mrs Alsop called from the kitchen, and the pair returned to the table in awkward silence.

'You'd better keep an eye on Polly, Mrs Alsop,' Bailey whispered in the cook's ear. 'I think she has feelings for the slave.'

'I've had the same thought myself, Mr Bailey,' Mrs Alsop said. 'I don't know what's gone wrong with that girl. She's a constant worry to me.'

Without a word, Polly stood and took herself back into the

scullery, parking herself right next to Barthold once more.

'My father spent some time in Africa,' she began, 'a place called Senegal, I think.'

Barthold suddenly raised his head as if to speak, but instead just stared deeply into Polly's beautiful pale-blue eyes, as she explained that in 1819, her father, Seamus Holmes, was part of the Royal African Corps, a scratch army of criminals and undesirables. His Battalion was sent to defend the Isle of Goree, in the Dakar region of Senegal, but due to their poor behaviour, the island's inhabitants campaigned to have them removed, and they were eventually disbanded in 1821.

'He said it was a beautiful country,' she continued, 'with wide, open plains, white sandy beaches and a sea as blue as a sapphire. He told me he saw long-necked giraffes, hippopotamuses and even an elephant. Can you imagine that?'

'Polly!' Mrs Alsop yelled from the kitchen. 'If you don't get back here and eat this pudding before it gets cold, I'll give it to Mr Bailey.'

'I'll have to go,' Polly sighed. 'Those two are watching everything I do, and they don't like me spending time with you. We rise early here, five-thirty in the morning, so I'll see you then. Sleep tight, dear Barthold, and watch the bed bugs don't bite.'

After they'd finished eating pudding, Bailey waited for the women to leave the kitchen before grabbing his chance to pounce on the slave, pinning him up hard against the scullery wall and hissing menacingly in his ear.

'Keep your eyes off Polly,' he warned, 'understand? She's not for the likes of you. Oh, and don't forget, I'm the head butler around here, and hell will freeze over before I allow the master to replace me with a black monkey like you, got it? Yes, that's right, you know exactly what I'm saying. You're not as dumb as you look, are you?'

Mr Strome was sitting in his tall, brown leather easy chair, trying to balance the thin-framed reading glasses on the end of his nose as he unfolded the latest edition of the Liverpool Chronicle. Mrs Strome and Miss Sarah were doing needlework on the sofa opposite, while Barthold was stood in the corner of the room, waiting on in his smart new clothing.

'Cup of tea, anyone?' Strome asked, lowering his newspaper.

'Yes please,' Mrs Strome answered. 'Would you like a cup of tea, Sarah?'

'Yes please, Mummy.'

'Very good,' Strome turned to Barthold. 'Be a good chap and pour three cups of tea, would you?'

Barthold looked nervous as he went over to a side table and poured the tea, unaware that behind the smiles and pleasantries of the seemingly idyllic family scene that was playing out before him, Mrs Strome harboured a deep grudge against her husband. She saw him as a man who was not driven to truly succeed in business, being too laidback to ever seize upon opportunities to further raise their station. She had always had a taste for the finer things in life, and though he would often characterise her as a malcontent, she saw nothing wrong in wanting a better lifestyle than the one that was currently being provided for her. This was perhaps owing to the fact that despite carrying herself as a lady, Agnes Strome, nee Barrett, was very much working class by birth. At around the age of nineteen, she came to understand that by adding seduction to her flourishing natural beauty, she could snag herself a rich businessman, or any other man of suitable wealth, and ensure that she would never be poor ever again. Eventually, she settled on Colin Strome, who she later discovered was no fool, as he knew exactly what she was and what she wanted, but decided to accept it on the grounds that he considered himself a plain, unattractive man, and was thus grateful to have such an attractive prize on his arm.

'Did I tell you,' she said, 'the Morgans are going into the sugar cane business?'

'Oh?' Strome raised his eyebrows. 'I thought Edmund was content exporting scrap iron.'

'Well, Marjorie says sugar is where the big money is these days, or so I'm told.'

'To hear Edmund tell it, he was already making a small fortune in scrap.'

'A small fortune, yes. Marjorie says you can earn between fifteen to twenty shillings per hundredweight of sugar. Not to mention, it's a much more prestigious industry than scrap metal, wouldn't you agree, darling?'

'Um.'

'Marjorie says that they might set up a business on St Kitts or the Isle of Nevis, wherever they are.'

'Both Caribbean Islands, my dear,' Strome said, returning to his newspaper.

'Ah, the Caribbean,' Mrs Strome sighed. 'I believe it's just simply beautiful out there.'

'Can we go there, Daddy?' Sarah chimed in.

'Um.'

'Would you not consider it, darling?' Mrs Strome probed.

'Well, I imagine it's quite lovely, but it'd be an awfully long journey to make for just a holiday.'

'No, I don't mean for a holiday, silly. Would you not consider going into the sugar cane business yourself?'

'Good Lord, no,' Strome scoffed at the idea.

'Why not? After all, we're barely making a living out of cotton.'

'Trust me, darling, it would be a foolhardy endeavour.'

'And why is that?'

'Because you can only farm fifty to three hundred acres, due to the Caribbean islands being so small. If I were to enter the sugar cane business, it would have to be in America, where you can farm on a much larger scale.'

'Well then, let's move to America. The demand for sugar is rising exponentially all across Europe, and there is just so much money to be made.'

'Oh yes, America,' Sarah clasped her hands together. 'Can we go, Daddy? Can we?'

'No, we can't, darling,' Strome laughed. 'We're doing perfectly alright here.'

'But we could be doing better,' Mrs Strome sniped.

'Well, it just so happens that Captain Walker is coming around tomorrow,' Strome said offhandedly.

'Walker?'

'Yes.'

'James Walker?'

'Yes.'

'Coming here? Whatever for?'

'He's coming with a cotton trader. They want to discuss the possibility of a joint venture that would make us all very rich.'

Agitated now, Mrs Strome put down her needlework and paused for a moment before speaking.

'Captain Walker is nothing more than a pirate,' she said. 'He is not to be trusted.'

'You've never liked him, have you, my dear?'

'No, I haven't. He's a rapscallion with neither money nor ambition.'

'Rubbish! He owns a heavy three-masted brigantine that can hold up to ninety slaves, so I'm told.'

'Oh, so we're going into the slave trade, are we? Is that what you're saying?'

'Certainly not. Everyone knows that slavery was outlawed in 1807.'

'Yes, and everyone also knows that it's still alive and well, thanks chiefly to the Liverpool merchants and town councillors.'

'More rubbish!'

'I believe it was you who told me that no fewer than sixty-four petitions were submitted by the Liverpool merchants and councillors to the House of Commons, asking for the abolition to be overturned.'

Strome folded and placed his newspaper down onto his lap, and then unhooked the thin-framed reading glasses from his nose and looked directly at his wife.

'That was a long time ago now,' he said. 'I'm simply stating that the captain is solvent, that's all.'

'You've always been a soft touch, Colin. No good will come of this venture, I can assure you.'

'Captain Walker is a man of integrity, my dear.'

'Well, when everything goes to hell, I promise not to say I told you so.'

There came a light tap on the door, as Bailey entered the room.

'Pardon the intrusion, sir,' he said, 'but Lieutenant Miles is here to see Miss Sarah.'

'Bring him in, Mr Bailey,' Strome replied. 'Bring him in. Oh, and Bailey.'

'Yes, sir?'

'How's it going with the scriptures?' Strome asked, glancing at

Barthold.

'Well, sir, I'm sorry to say it, but the slave is a dullard. He's completely unteachable.'

Agnes burst into laughter. She had warned her husband that the slave was nothing more than an animal, and that he could not be tamed.

'So much for the scriptures taking the beast out of him,' she chuckled.

'Unteachable, you say?' Strome, said trying to ignore his wife's howls.

'I'm afraid he doesn't know a psalm from a sandwich, sir.'

'Very well, Bailey. You tried your best, I suppose.'

'Yes, sir. Thank you, sir.'

Lieutenant Laurance Miles presented in full dress uniform, and stood at such a height that he had to stoop and remove his tall black Shako hat – which carried the large, round brass badge of the First Royal Regiment of Foot – and tuck it smartly under his right arm as he passed under the doorframe. He wore a bright-red, high-necked tunic bearing large golden epaulettes, and tight-fitting black trousers with a single red stripe running down the outside of each leg. He was twenty years old, and kept his black hair short and parted in the middle, and his moustache well trimmed, as befitted the scion of a wealthy family who lived in what could only be described as a small mansion overlooking Sefton Park. In short, he was privileged, vain and arrogant, and a dandy to be sure.

'Mr Strome, Mrs Strome, Sarah,' he offered his greetings, bowing to each of them in turn.

'Ah, Laurence, please join us,' Strome gestured for their guest to take a seat.'

'Apologies for any inconvenience, Mr Strome, but I'm due to

leave for the West Indies soon,' Laurence explained, 'and I wish to see your daughter before we set sail.'

'You're always welcome in this house, my boy.'

'Thank you, sir,' Laurence bowed again.

'We were only just talking about the Caribbean, weren't we, Daddy?' Sarah said.

'Indeed, but don't be getting any ideas about us going there, my dear.'

'Once you and Laurence are married, you can settle there if you wish, darling,' Mrs Strome suggested.

'Oh, Laurence, will you take me with you?' Sarah asked.

'Of course, my dearest Sarah,' Laurence smiled, 'but we will need to marry at the nearest opportunity. Only then can we settle down in the west indies.'

'Will you take tea, Laurence?' Mrs Strome asked.

'That would be lovely, Mrs Strome,' he answered.

'Please, call me Agnes.'

'Yes, tea would be lovely, Agnes.'

'Barthold, a cup of tea for the lieutenant, if you please.

Mrs Strome clicked her fingers, and Barthold duly obliged.

'I see you have acquired a black servant, Mr Strome,' Laurence observed.

'Yes, to hear Sarah tell it, it's the latest fashion.

'Indeed, sir. We will have many black servants in the West Indies,' Laurence winked at his fiancée.

'He's a mute,' Mrs Strome said, her distain for Barthold evident.

'I beg your pardon?'

'My husband has bought us a mute.'

'I'm sorry, Agnes, but I don't understand.'

'No, neither do I, Laurance. Neither do I.'

'My wife is referring to Barthold,' Strome interjected. 'I got him very cheap, you see, because he cannot speak.'

'How extraordinary,' Laurence raised his eyebrows, 'and also most beneficial, I would think.

'How so?' Mrs Strome asked, annoyance in her voice.

'Well, it means he will follow instructions without complaint, don't you agree?'

'So, I see you've joined the First Royal Regiment of Foot,' Strome moved to change the subject.

'That is correct, sir. Sarah informs me that you have never served yourself, sir. Is that true?

'Unfortunately, yes, that is true. However, my father served with the Second Royal Regiment of Foot back in seventeen forty-five. He was transferred from Cork to the West Indies.'

'Funny how history has a habit of repeating itself, sir.'

'Indeed.'

As far as Strome was concerned, the young Lieutenant was ticking all the boxes as a potential suitor for his beloved daughter, and doing a fine job of ingratiating himself into the family.

'Didn't you ever consider a career in the military, sir?' Laurence asked.

'Alas, my father would not allow it,' Strome answered. 'He had other plans for me, you see.'

'That is a shame, sir. I'm sure you would have made a fine officer.'

'Yes, but what's done is done,' Strome mumbled into his teacup, again wishing to switch topics.

'Tell me, Laurence, do you intend to stay in the Army?' Mrs Strome asked.

'Oh yes, absolutely.'

'And what are your ambitions there?'

'Well, I hope to make captain by year's end, and then perhaps major the year after.'

'That's good to hear,' Mrs Strome said approvingly, 'isn't it, Colin?'

'Yes, good for you, Laurence,' Strome agreed. 'Jolly good.'

Mrs Strome allowed herself a satisfied smile, as she reflected on how close she was to finally achieving through her daughter what she had failed to do herself. Sarah was about to marry someone who was not only wealthy, but also driven to keep progressing further and further up the social ladder, unlike her own complacent husband.

'Shall we give the happy couple some time alone, my dear?' she said, beckoning her husband to follow as she rose from the sofa and headed for the door. 'You, too, Barthold. Come along.'

After a final exchange of pleasantries, the doting parents left their daughter and future son-in-law to say their goodbyes in private, with Miss Sarah sitting bolt upright, like a model posing for a portrait, in her lovely long royal-blue dress, and her thick strawberry-blonde hair tied back smartly in perfect ringlets. She kept her eyes lowered and declined to speak, pretending to be shy, and though Laurence could not help but sense the distance between them, he did not understand the cause of it; the truth being that Sarah was carrying the burden of a guilty secret, for not only was she not attracted to Laurence, she was actually lusting after the young slave Barthold, who she thought to be more manly, exotic and handsome.

'Do you mind if I smoke?' Laurence asked.

Sarah nodded her head slightly, and he reached down deep into his tunic pocket and produced a long, thick cigar, which filled the air with huge grey clouds of smoke as he began puffing away.

'You look very beautiful today,' he commented, but she did not respond, and instead continued to look down at her pale, delicate hands until he got up from his seat knelt down alongside her, covering her hand with his.

'Can I pour you a glass of my father's madeira?' she asked.

'No, thank you,' he said, before clearing his throat. 'Sarah, I've, um, taken the liberty of speaking to the army chaplain, and he has agreed to perform the wedding ceremony as soon as possible.'

'Oh,' she felt her stomach turn. 'You've thought of everything.'

'Of course,' he smiled. 'As an officer, it's my job to always be prepared.'

'Is that all this marriage is to you,' she said accusingly, pulling her hand away from his, 'some kind of military manoeuvre?'

'No, of course not,' he said, the colour draining from his face. 'Sarah, why are you acting so strange? Now that we're finally alone, you seem somewhat distracted.'

'I'm sorry, Laurence. It's just that I've suddenly become quite fatigued.'

'Oh, my darling, can I get you anything?'

'No, I'm quite alright now, thank you,' she smiled. 'I think it's passed.'

'My dearest Sarah,' he leaned in close to her, 'would you mind if I kissed you?'

'Yes, I would mind,' she pulled back from him. 'In fact, I think that it would be most inappropriate at this stage of our relationship.'

'But we're about to be married. Surely, one kiss wouldn't hurt, would it?

'Oh, alright,' she sighed. 'I suppose one kiss would be permissible – but just the one, I mean it.'

He moved towards her again, and they slowly embraced in a passionate kiss, only for Sarah to push away violently after feeling his hand grip tightly around her tiny waist, as somewhere in that foggy, immature mind, she felt that being intimate with the Lieutenant was a betrayal of her true love for Barthold.

'Sarah, what's wrong?' Laurence asked, getting increasingly more confused by his fiancée's seemingly erratic behaviour.

'Just because we're about to be married doesn't mean that you can take advantage of me.'

'Don't you – I thought you felt as I do? Ever since I first set eyes on you, all I've wanted was to be around you and to hold you, and to tell you that I will always love you. Don't you understand?'

'Oh, I understand perfectly, Laurence. I'm not some cheap whore that you can fawn over whenever your base impulses kick in. I'm a lady, and a lady does not behave in such a manner.'

'Of course, please forgive me, my love,' he leapt to his feet, face flushed with embarrassment. 'I let my passions run away with me. It won't happen again, I swear.'

'I will forgive you this once, Laurence. I mean, I'm not a complete idiot. I know that you are, after all, a man, and a man has his needs, but you must learn to control your urges while in my presence, understand?'

'Understood.'

Having left her daughter and the young lieutenant alone in the morning room, and with her husband en route to a business meeting at the offices of one of his associates, Mrs Strome was sitting in the back parlour with Barthold waiting on.

'Another cup of tea please, Barthold,' she ordered.

The slave obliged at once, but in his haste, he accidently spilled some of the hot tea onto the lady's crisp white table linen, sending her into a blind rage.

'Oh, look what you've done now, you imbecile!'

Quick as a flash, she was up and over to the mantlepiece, where she grabbed hold of a fire poker and began to beat young Barthold across the back

'Stupid nigger!' she screamed over and over, getting louder with each successive blow.

In all the commotion, neither she nor Barthold noticed Miss Sarah dashing into the room with Lt Laurence Miles at her side.

'Mummy, what are you doing?' Sarah cried. 'Stop!'

'Just look at what this idiot's gone and done!' Mrs Strome jabbed a pointed finger at the small brown stain. 'He's spilled tea all over my best tablecloth, but the bastard won't do it again, I can tell you.'

'He spilled some tea?' Sarah was incredulous. 'How on earth could you beat him over such a trivial thing?'

'You need to understand something about this creature, darling. He's no different than an animal, and when animals make a mess in the house, you rub their noses in it, so that they know not to do it again. He simply must be punished.'

Sarah placed a comforting hand on Barthold's shoulder, much to the annoyance of both her mother and her fiancée, with Laurence in particular being left dumbstruck by her concern for the slave's well-being.

'Why are you stroking that nappy hair of his?' Mrs Strome spat. 'He's not some pet Labrador, and besides, you don't know where he's been.'

'This must stop at once, Mummy,' Sarah yelled forcefully, her eyes burning with rage. 'You shall not harm him again.'

'When your father is out of this house, I give the orders around here, not you!'

'Please, Sarah, your mother is right,' Laurence added. 'Calm yourself at once.'

'Oh, shut up, Laurence,' Sarah shot back. 'Don't you have a boat to catch?'

'Well, I never!' the lieutenant shook his head in disbelief.

'You won't treat him like this anymore, Mummy,' Sarah continued. 'He's a human being, and he deserves our respect as much as Mrs Alsop or Mr Bailey or Polly.'

'I'm sure I don't like your tone, young lady,' Mrs Strome replied darkly.

'And I'm sure you'll have to get used to it if this sort of behaviour doesn't stop.'

'Oh, just get out, the lot of you,' Mrs Strome screeched, eyes ablaze.

'Come along, Barthold,' Sarah linked arms with the shellshocked slave, who hadn't moved an inch since the moment Mrs Strome started hitting him. 'You can wait on the lieutenant and I back in the morning room.'

Mrs Alsop was busy rolling out dough to make bread with, whilst Polly and Kwento were sitting at the large oak dining table, when Kwento pointed towards the stove in a warning gesture, only for Mrs Alsop to ignore him as usual.

'And I said to Mrs Molloy,' the cook went on chatting, 'if you're serious about going into service, you must first do your homework and find yourself a decent household, I said.'

Kwento became more animated in his waving and gesturing, moving his arm up and down in a more urgent manner.

'Will you please put your arm down and stop flapping it around like a headless chicken!' Mrs Alsop barked.

'Mrs Alsop,' Polly croaked, but was also ignored.

'Anyway, I said to Mrs Molloy that we were most fortunate to be in this household because–'

'Mrs Alsop!' Polly said again, more firmly this time.

'Will you stop interrupting, child! And don't take on so–'

'Mrs Alsop, the stove is on fire.'

'Oh, hell and bluster! Why didn't you say something? Don't just sit there like a pair of bookends, the pair of you, help me!'

She threw open the stove door and tried to remove the baking tray, while Polly tried to fan the smoke away with a tea towel.

'Oh, Mrs Alsop,' Polly coughed, 'them buns are burnt to cinders!'

'I can see that, Polly,' Mrs Alsop shouldered past her and dumped the ruined delicacies on the sideboard. 'They're blacker than that useless get Barthold, dearie me.'

'It's not his fault, Mrs Alsop. He did try to warn you.'

'What do you mean, tried to warn me? He can't speak a word of the King's, the black devil.'

There was a tapping at the tradesmen's entrance, down in the front stairwell, where a shadowy figure stood silhouetted against the frosted-glass-panelled door.

'Who the devil can that be?' Mrs Alsop wondered aloud. 'Go answer it, Polly. Go on, girl, quickly now!'

As Polly went to answer the door, Bailey appeared holding a tray with one hand while wafting the remnants of billowing black smoke with the other.

'Oh dear,' he laughed, 'what's happened here, Mrs Alsop?'

'Blacky here made me burn them buns is all,' she shot Barthold a sideways glance. 'Anyway, what can I do for you, Mr Bailey?'

'The master has requested a fresh pot of tea.'

'I'm afraid you'll have to make it yourself, Mr Bailey. I'm all fingers and thumbs at the moment, as you can see.'

'Of course, Mrs Alsop,' Bailey chuckled amiably. 'No problem at all.'

Polly re-entered the kitchen, followed by a swarthy-looking

gentleman wearing a tatty grey overcoat and brown bowler hat, who was carrying what looked to be a large brown sack over his shoulder. This was Mr Kelly, a thickset fellow with a drinker's nose and a permanent five o'clock shadow, and an old friend of Bailey's. Upon seeing Mrs Alsop, he quickly removed his bowler hat to reveal a mop of black, greasy unkempt hair.

'A grand mornin' to ya, Mary,' Kelly said, in a thick Irish brogue. 'and may I be so bold as to say how beautiful yer lookin' dis mornin'.'

'That's Mrs Alsop to you, if you don't mind,' came a grumbled reply.

She had had many past dealings with Kelly, and was not overly fond of him to say the least.

'What can I do for you, Mr Kelly?' she asked.

'Eamon! Good to see you, man,' Bailey cut in, gesturing towards the table with an open hand. 'Here, please come and sit down.'

'Oh, I'll not be stoppin' long, Edward,' Kelly said.

'Thank God for that,' Mrs Alsop muttered under her breath.

'Polly, be a dear and pour Mr Kelly a nice cup of tea, would you?' Bailey said, rubbing his hands together. 'Oh, and then if you could take a pot upstairs to the master while you're at it, there's a good girl.'

'Ahem,' Mrs Alsop folded her arms under her bosom. 'Excuse me, but I give the orders down here, Mr Bailey.'

'But of course,' Bailey offered a sickly smile, 'I meant no disrespect, Mrs. Alsop.'

'Shall I bring out a plate of your delicious homemade macaroons, Mrs Alsop?' Polly asked.

'No, that won't be necessary,' Mrs Alsop answered. 'Mr Kelly isn't stopping long.'

Kelly dropped the heavy sack onto the kitchen table with a loud thump, and then leaned forward to whisper to Bailey.

'Um, Edward,' he said, glancing around furtively, 'yer do know der's a sambo standing in d' corner of dis room, don't ya?'

'Yes, that's Barthold,' Bailey replied, 'the master's new house boy.'

'Boy?' Kelly exclaimed. 'He's got to be twenty-five years old if he's a day!'

'Oh, stop exaggerating, Kelly,' Mrs Alsop tutted.

Polly poured Kelly a strong, sweet cup of tea and placed it down on the table, minus the macaroons, and then left with a full pot for the master.

'So, Eamon, how's Bridget?' Bailey asked.

'Oh, she's doin' just fine,' Kelly said, 'tanks for askin'. She's just started a new job at d' tallow factory, ya know, d' one just off Scotland Road der.'

'Well, that's good news, isn't it, Mrs. Alsop?'

'If you say so, Mr Bailey,' Mrs Alsop shrugged. 'Mr Kelly, kindly remove whatever that is from my table, if you please.'

'But I've brought dis for you, missus.'

'For me?'

'For you, me lovely,' Kelly winked. 'Ya know, Mrs Alsop, if I wusn't a married man, I'd make ya mine for sure, I would.'

'Mr Kelly!' Mrs Alsop exploded. 'This is a decent house. Please keep a civil tongue in your head!'

'So, what's inside the sack, Eamon?' Bailey jumped in, hoping to diffuse the situation.

'Why, a half pig, Edward,' Kelly smiled broadly.

'A half pig?' Mrs Alsop threw up her hands. 'Search the Holly book! What the hell would we want with a half pig. Get it off my table right now. Heavens knows where it's been!'

'I got it cheap, so I did,' Kelly explained, 'from a mate who works at d' abattoir.'

'What, and you thought you could offload it here?' Mrs Alsop blazed. 'I'll have none of your contraband in my kitchen. You can take it right back to wherever you got it from.

'Now, don't be so hasty, missus. I can give it to ya for a good price.

While all this was going on, Polly quietly returned from upstairs and took a seat at the table, leaning her chin into her hands as she attempted to catch up on what she had missed.

'I get my meat from Mr Thompson,' Mrs Alsop said haughtily, 'a reputable butcher on the high street, thank you very much.'

'Oh aye,' Kelly laughed, 'and I bet he gets it from d' same place I do.'

'I beg your pardon?'

'Mrs Alsop,' Bailey interjected again, 'if it is indeed a good price, what harm would it do to buy from someone else on this occasion?'

'You can save your breath,' Mrs Alsop shut him down at once, 'I'm not interested.'

'It does look a nice cut, Mrs Alsop,' Polly observed, examining the contents of the open sack.

'And who asked you?'

'I'm just saying–'

'Oh, shut up, Polly.'

'Well, I tried my best, my old mate,' Bailey said to his friend.

'Ah, never mind,' Kelly picked up the sack and slung it over his shoulder. 'I'll flog it down d' pub tonight, so I will. Now, I must be away.'

'Very well, Eamon, but don't leave it so long next time, eh?'

'Polly, kindly show Mr Kelly out,' Mrs Alsop said. 'There's a good girl.'

'Yes, Mrs Alsop.'

That night, Polly was the last of the staff to retire to bed, and after finishing up her work in the kitchen, she went into the scullery with a cup of hot cocoa for Kwento.

'Well, what a day we've had today, eh? There was Mrs Alsop, dashing around the kitchen like a demented cow, while smoke bellowed out everywhere,' she laughed. 'Then, there was me waving the dish cloth all around, and you standing there like a right lemon! Oh, I must say, it was so funny.'

Sitting down alongside him on his cot, she took hold of his hand and gave it a gentle squeeze. This came as a great surprise to Kwento, who had never experienced intimacy with a white woman before. In fact, the only contact of any kind that he had experienced with whites had always ended in aggression or violence, but after his initial sense of trepidation passed, he began to find the warmth of Polly's hand to be most pleasant.

'Oh, sweet Barthold,' she said sadly, 'if only you could talk. I want to know more about you. I want to know who you are and where you came from, but you can never tell, and that makes me feel very upset indeed.'

Suddenly, and very much unexpectedly, Miss Sarah entered the scullery, and instantly became furious at the site of Polly and Kwento holding hands.

'Polly, what the hell do you think you are doing, you filthy girl?' she screamed.

'Sorry, Miss Sarah,' Polly stumbled to her feet. 'I only–'

'Get out!'

'I meant no harm, Miss Sarah,' Polly wept, 'I swear.'

'I don't know what you were thinking, you stupid girl. Just get out, and I don't want to see you in here ever again, do you understand?'

'Yes, Miss Sarah.'

A sobbing Polly dashed out of the scullery, leaving Kwento alone with Miss Sarah. The young lady then took a chair and braced the door from the inside, before turning to face a very confused and concerned Kwento.

'I'm so disappointed in you, Barthold,' she said. 'Very disappointed. For some stupid reason, I expected more from you. Did you know that it was I who argued that you should remain in this house? I even went against my own mother on your behalf, and look how you repay me, with treachery. I deserve better than this.'

Kwento's confusion only grew as Miss Sarah began to jump up and down, stamping her feet like a spoilt child, before suddenly becoming calm again and sitting down on the edge of the cot. She was silent for quite some time, until she eventually began slowly stroking Kwento's hair , while humming to herself in a low voice. She then started inching closer and closer to him, staring deep into his chocolate-brown eyes.

'Oh, Barthold,' she giggled, 'you know I can't stay mad at you for long. When I look into those gorgeous big brown eyes, well, my heart just starts to melt. I must confess that you really do affect me so.'

She covered her mouth slightly with her hand as she began to giggle again, and it soon became apparent to Kwento that the girl was clearly feeble-minded. This worried him greatly as, being only a slave, he would have to obey whatever orders he received from one of the ladies of the house, even one who was madly attracted to him because he possessed all the qualities that one looked for in a man: ruggedly handsome, with a great physique moulded by years of hard labour.

Kwento's concerns were doubling by the second, as Miss Sarah pressed right up against him, and though her beauty was undeniable, he knew that he could never feel love for her. She was privilege made manifest, a bodily representation of the very system that had stolen his freedom, knowing nothing of the hardship and fear that had defined his life since the day he was captured by Mustafa. It was in this moment that he realised for the first time that he was actually in love with Polly, a working-class girl whose background was more relatable.

The two women were as far apart in appearance as they were in station. Miss Sarah was tall and slender, with perfectly-styled blonde hair, whereas Polly was of average height, redheaded and 'heavy-boned,' as her mother used to put it.

'You've been a very naughty boy, but I'm willing to let you make it up to me just this once,' Miss Sarah continued. 'You know, the fact that you can't speak excites me very much, as I know that whatever happens here in this room will always remain our little secret.'

Getting up and leaning over him, she began to remove his shirt before pushing him down onto the cot and unbuttoning her blouse, letting it fall slowly to the floor and revealing her perfect pale hourglass figure, as the tiny, claustrophobic room quickly filled with the sweet, sickly scent of her perfume. She then removed the slide pin from her strawberry-blonde hair and shook her head from side to side, allowing the long tresses to unfold around her soft, white, slender neck and shoulders. Kwento became very uneasy, as his mind raced back to the plantation near Knoxville. He remembered a black overseer named Gorgeous Pete, who was the master's champion because he had fathered sixteen children to four slave girls, only to later fall out of favour after being found in bed with Eleanor Cunliffe, the master's wife. For that, he was dragged from the house and beaten, and then hanged from the nearest tree.

Kwento turned his head away, not wanting to engage, but Miss

Sarah was not to be denied. She reached out a thin, trembling hand to touch his glistening bare brown chest, and though he tensed up at her touch, this only served to increase her excitement, and strengthen her resolve to seize this chance at finally exploring her sexuality. Up to that point, she had only experienced awkward, childish fumbles on her mother's sofa with her fiancée, Lieutenant Laurence Miles, and now she was ready to feel like a real woman by satisfying her woman's needs. Plus, beneath her immature proclamations about loving the slave, there was a deeper part of her that viewed him as merely a piece of property owned by her family, thus making him hers to do with as she pleased, and after gently gliding her delicate fingers across his muscular body, she then proceeded to mount and ride him like one of the prized black Arab stallions that continued to haunt his dreams.

Ecstasy surged through her veins like bolts of lightning, and she arched her back slightly as she gripped his torso with both hands. Meanwhile, Kwento fixed his gaze on the damp, bare brick wall, desperately trying to block out what was going on, but finding it increasingly difficult. For all her feigning innocence, it was quite clear to Kwento by Miss Sarah's way and manner that she was indeed promiscuous and that this was not her first sexual encounter. He tried his best to think only of his beautiful, dear, sweet Polly, but it was no use, as Miss Sarah began to thrust hard and fast with her narrow hips, heightening his senses and bring him closer to his relief. He clenched his teeth and grimaced, but the temptation was far too great, and in the end, he had no choice other than to yield to his basic primal instincts, cupping Miss Sarah's small, firm breasts in both hands as they became locked together tightly, entwined in a lover's embrace, and it was not long before they both reached a loud and shuddering climax.

As soon as it was over, Miss Sarah jumped up and dressed quickly. She then left the scullery without a word, though not before stopping in the doorway to glance back at Kwento's glistening sweat-soaked body. He was completely spent, both physically and emotionally, and as he rolled on to his side, a single tear trickled down his cheek. Already, he was wracked with guilt, feeling as though he had not only let himself down, but that, more importantly, he had also betrayed Polly.

I should have done more to stop it, he thought. I should have shown more restraint.

In truth, there was little he could have done. Miss Sarah was, after all, a lady of the house, and he was just a slave.

MY NAME IS KWENTO

Kwento was waiting on Mrs Strome as she sat reading on an ox-blood chesterfield sofa, when Bailey entered the parlour.

'Captain Walker to see you, madam,' the butler announced.

'Well, don't just stand there,' Mrs Strome looked up from her book, 'bring him in.'

'Yes, madam,' Bailey bowed.

The first thing Captain Walker did upon entering was glance across at Kwento, before removing his tatty black tricorn hat, which it seemed nobody had told him was well out of fashion. Otherwise, Walker cut a fine figure in his long, dark navy-blue jacket and knee-length black leather boots. He had a stern, weather-beaten face, but remained quite handsome for a man of middle age, and it was noticeable how urgently Mrs Strome composed herself and fixed her hair, having seemed to light up once in his presence.

'Captain Walker,' she smiled, 'you're early.'

'Yes, I hope it's no inconvenience,' he bowed slightly.

'Not at all, please sit down. My husband is out at the moment. He won't be back for at least another hour.'

'Oh, that's alright. Gives us more time to talk.'

'More time to talk about what, Captain Walker?'

'Oh, just things, Mrs Strome.

'Very well. Will you take tea, Captain?'

'That would be nice, thank you.'

'Barthold, tea for the captain please.'

Barthold hesitated at first, before carefully walking over to the small side table and pouring the tea. As he did so, he and Walker locked eyes in a stare that neither was willing to break.

'Barthold?' the captain laughed, shooing Kwento back into the corner. 'I know him as Stowy.'

'You mean to say that you know this wretch?'

'I should think so, yes. He sailed with me from America as a stowaway, hence the name.'

'I'm confused.'

'It's quite simple really. He boarded my ship whilst we were docked in New York.'

'New York? He's from New York?'

'Well, not exactly,' Walker grinned sardonically. 'We think he came from somewhere else.'

'Where, then?'

'Well, when an African flees his master and arrives at the docks, he could have come from any of the southern states, so one can never be too sure, you understand?

'Whatever the case, I must tell you, Captain, that I hate all Africans. They're stupid, lazy and indolent, the lot of them.'

'I rather disagree. I find that once you get to know them, they can really grow on you.

'We shall have to agree to disagree, I think. Anyway, let's change the subject, shall we? Where is your business partner?'

'Oh, Mr Carter will be here shortly. I came a little early, remember.'

'Of course.'

Then, to Kwento's complete and utter amazement, Captain Walker stood up, strode over to Mrs Strome and sat himself down beside her, placing his right hand on her right thigh. For her part, the lady looked almost as bewildered as her young slave.

'Why, Captain Walker, what are you doing?' she cried.

'Oh, how I've missed you, Agnes,' he said.

'Please, James, not in front of the servant.'

'Don't worry about Stowy, he's a mute. He hardly knows what day it is.'

'You're right, of course. I remember Bailey saying that he doesn't know a psalm from a sandwich,' she laughed.

'Have you missed me?'

'What a silly question.'

'Well, have you?'

'Of course I have, but it's… difficult.'

'How so?'

'I'm a married woman, James.'

'What are you saying – that we go on just snatching moments together, hiding in doorways or meeting in parks. Is that it?'

'That's not fair, James, and you know it. Did you really think that I would leave Colin?

'Foolishly, I did.'

'I've told you before, I will never divorce him,' she began to weep. 'I've too much to lose.'

'Forgive me for upsetting you, my dear. That was not my intention. It's simply that I love you, and I want to spend the rest of my life with you. Is that so wrong?'

He took her hand in his, at which point Kwento decided that it may be prudent to fix his gaze on his shiny black shoes.

'There's nothing wrong with loving someone,' she whispered, 'but when that person is married…'

Walker stood and walked over to the large bay window that overlooked Abercromby Park, while Mrs Strome took a small white handkerchief from her sleeve and used it to pinch her nose.

'This whole affair was a moment of madness,' she said. 'We we're never supposed to fall in love.'

'So, where does this leave us, my dearest Agnes?

'Back where we started, I suppose.'

'You won't divorce him, then?'

'Please, James, don't make me go over this again.'

'I may have a solution.'

'A solution?'

'What if your husband were to meet with an… accident?'

'An accident? I'm not sure I like where this is going, James.'

Kwento took a deep breath and swallowed hard, as he, too, didn't like where this was going. He could not believe what he was hearing, but dared not remove his gaze from the floor, for fear of revealing that he fully understood everything that was being said.

'Just hear me out, my dear,' Walker said. 'If he were to be killed whilst visiting, let's say, the Coburg Dock, that would leave you free to marry again.'

'Indeed it would, but I have two questions.'

'Go on...'

'Firstly, why would my husband ever find himself at the Coburg Dock? And secondly, how would he be killed?'

'He would be invited to the dock by myself, and once there, he would meet with a terrible accident, being struck by either a horse and cart or a loose bail falling from a derrick.'

'Well, it would seem that you have everything worked out, James, but what if you should fail? I would be left to nurse a cripple for the rest of my life. Have you thought about that?'

'Nothing will go wrong, my sweet. You'll just have to trust me.'

'Oh, I certainly do trust that you know what you're doing, James. You're one of the most ruthless men I have ever met, who will stop at nothing until you get exactly what you want.'

'And if I'm not mistaken, that's exactly what attracts you to me, is it not?'

'I must confess, that side of you does excite me, yes.'

'Just as your beauty excites me, my dearest – with a passion that you cannot imagine.'

'I don't want him to suffer,' she said quietly. 'It must be quick, agreed?'

'Agreed.'

'I'm not a complete bitch, you know?'

'The thought never crossed my mind.'

Then, as if on cue, the door opened and Mr Strome entered the room.

'Ah, James,' he said amiably, handing his hat to Kwento, 'I see you're early.'

'Yes, I hope that's alright?' Walker replied.

'Oh, but of course. I trust my wife has kept you entertained?'

Kwento couldn't help but glance over at Mrs Strome, who had turned her head away from her husband.

'Ahem, yes,' Walker coughed, 'she has been most accommodating. You're a very lucky man, sir.

'Well, gentlemen, if you'll excuse me, I'm sure you have much to discuss,' Mrs Strome said, still blushing as she made a hurried exit.

'Please, have a seat,' Strome gestured towards the sofa his wife had just vacated. 'May I offer you a drink?'

'Your wife was kind enough to offer me tea.'

'I was thinking of something a little stronger. Barthold, two whiskies please,' Strome grinned, as Kwento move swiftly towards the drinks cabinet and set about pouring and serving. 'So, when is your merchant friend arriving?'

'He should be here quite soon, I expect.'

'Cigar?'

'No, thank you,' Walker waved away the offer.

'Jolly good,' Strome lit one up and started puffing it to life. 'Now, what can you tell me about Mr…'

'Carter. I've known Steven for quite some time. He's of noble character, and owns two cotton mills in Manchester.'

'Is he experienced?'

'Oh yes, he has great knowledge of the cotton industry, and also many contacts.'

'I looking forward to meeting him, then.'

'Indeed.'

'Another whisky?'

'Forgive me, but I remain an old sea dog at heart. I don't suppose there's any rum in that cabinet?' Walker said raising his empty glass.

'Certainly.'

Strome was directing Kwento back to the drinks cabinet when the door sprung open and Bailey entered once again.

'A Mr Carter to see you, sir,' the Butler said.

'Perfect timing,' Strome said. 'Please bring him in, would you?'

'Yes, sir.'

Carter was a small, thin man with narrow, shifty eyes and a pinched nose, whose tightly-stretched skin gave him a sallow complexion, and at a glance, Kwento was suspicious that he was not quite the wealthy, well-connected man that Walker professed him to be. He was supposedly the owner of two cotton mills, yet the cuffs on his brown winter coat were noticeably frayed at the edges, suggesting a distinct lack of money.

'Barthold,' Strome disturbed Kwento from his thoughts, 'a drink for Mr Carter. What would you like, sir?

'Um, a whisky would be nice, thanks,' Carter said, removing his hat.

'Please, call me Colin,' Strome said.

'Thank you, Colin,' Carter bowed slightly.

'Barthold, a whisky for Mr Carter.'

'Please, call me Steven.'

'Thank you, Steven,' Strome smiled, evidently in high spirits. 'Now, gentlemen, to business. James tells me that you have two cotton mills in Manchester, Steven. Is that correct?'

'Aye, that's correct,' Carter said. 'I own two water-powered mills in the Ancoats district.'

'Jolly good.'

'Steven has a proposal for you, Colin,' Walker said, as though prompting his associate.

'Uh, yes,' Carter said, after receiving and draining his whisky in one gulp. 'I have reliable contacts in America, and they have advised me that the Graton plantation in Louisiana is a solid investment opportunity.'

'Is that so?' Strome stroked his chin.

'The word is that the land is fertile and produces high-grade cotton,' Carter said.

'This is something I've been able to corroborate through my own contacts,' Walked added, 'but of course, any potential profit is dependent on the amount of investment.

'Which brings us to the subject of money,' Strome raised an eyebrow.

'Indeed,' Walker nodded. 'Steven and I have agreed to commit the sum of one thousand guineas each to fund this project, but to make it work–'

'You need me to invest a thousand guineas, too?'

'Correct.'

'And what sort of return could I expect to see on this amount?'

'Well, if projections are accurate,' Carter said, 'we can expect to at least treble our investment. James and I are both in agreement that it's as close to a sure thing as could be, but the final decision must ultimately be yours, Colin.'

'Yes, of course.'

Mrs Alsop was sitting at the kitchen table wearing a light-pink single-buttoned overall and a white floppy bonnet, drumming her thick, flour-covered fingers against the hard oak surface while she waited for Polly to arrive. She seemed on edge, distracted, and kept looking up at the large wooden-framed clock that was ticking loudly on the wall opposite. She and Bailey were fully aware that Miss Sarah had been visiting the scullery late each evening, ever since she had caught Polly and Barthold together, but being powerless to stop these late night liaisons, they said nothing.

'Sit down, Polly,' Mrs Alsop said, as the young housekeeper entered the room. 'I need to have a word with you.'

'Is something wrong, Mrs Alsop?' Polly asked.

'As a matter of fact, there is. Earlier today, I was summoned by Miss Sarah, and let me tell you, she was not happy.'

'Wasn't happy? Why?'

'She said that she wants you out of the house immediately.'

'Why, what have I done?' Polly's mouth fell open. 'I don't understand.'

'You were caught being intimate with blacky, weren't you, you silly child.'

'His name is Barthold, Mrs Alsop, not blacky. He's a human being, just like me and you.

'Oh, you're truly lost, my girl. He's obviously worked his dark magic on you good and proper.'

'But I've done nothing wrong, Mrs Alsop. We were only holding hand is all, I swear.'

'I told you when he first arrived, when he was stood right here in this very kitchen, to keep away from him, but no, you just wouldn't listen, would you?'

Polly dropped down onto a chair with a thud, and then lowered her head into her hands and began to weep uncontrollably.

'Oh, Mrs. Alsop, what am I going to do?' she sobbed. 'I need this job. What will I tell my mother and father? You know my father's been discharged from the army, don't you?'

'I didn't know that, Polly. You've never discussed your parents with me, but I'm sorry to hear it, truly I am.'

'Dad was speared in the legs while he was out in Africa, you see. He has to walk on crutches now, and mother's been very poorly and had to give up work in the wash house, so they rely on me to put food on the table. Oh, Mrs Alsop, what am I going to do?'

Polly's parents had, along with many of their compatriots, arrived in Liverpool from Galway, on the west coast of Ireland, in 1800, in search of a better life for themselves and their families.

'There, there, now,' Mrs Alsop put an arm around Polly's shoulder, 'don't go upsetting yourself. You'll not be the first to have made a mistake in life, believe me.

'I suppose I'd better get packing,' Polly tried to pull herself together. 'You did say that Miss Sarah wants me out immediately, didn't you?

'Yes, child, that's what she said.'

Mrs Alsop offered Polly her crisp white handkerchief, and after using it to wipe away the tears that had been streaming from her eyes, Polly got to her feet with as much poise and dignity as she could muster. She had always tried her very best to please Mrs Alsop, despite the older woman's constant efforts to put her down, so from her point of view, the one positive was that she wouldn't have to see the old battleaxe ever again. Mrs Alsop, on the other hand, saw herself as someone who knew her job inside and out, having been in continuous service for more than twenty years following the break-up of her marriage to Mr John Alsop, a Lancashire coal miner, with whom she had a son, Michael. The relationship had failed due to John's heavy drinking and routine infidelity, all of which became too much for Mrs Alsop, who as an act of punishment, insisted upon separation without a formal divorce. She had always considered herself to be a firm but fair woman, but when it came to her estranged husband, fairness went straight out the window.

'And where do you think you're going, young miss?' Mrs Alsop asked, stopping Polly in her tracks.

'To pack my clothes,' Polly answered.

'Oh, sit down, you silly girl.'

'Mrs Alsop, I don't–'

'Now, you listen to me and listen good. Miss Sarah was very cross with you, very cross indeed, but I managed to calm her down and persuaded her to give you one more chance, so stop your crying.'

'Oh, thank you so much, Mrs Alsop. How can I ever repay you?'

'You can repay me by staying away from Blacky – I mean,

Barthold.'

'Oh, I promise, it will never happen again, Mrs Alsop.'

'There's a good girl. Now, get that dolly tub out and get washing the master's clothes.

'Yes, of course, Mrs Alsop,' Polly smiled.

Strome shook hands enthusiastically with his new business partners, Captain James Walker and Mr Steven Carter, and bade a warm farewell before Mr Bailey led them out of the house. Then, with Kwento there waiting on him, he relaxed into his big easy chair and reflected on a meeting that had concluded with him agreeing to invest the huge sum of one thousand guineas in the Graton plantation, as he sat smiling with a whisky in one hand and a fat, stubby cigar in the other.

'Well, Barthold,' he said, 'that went rather well, don't you think?'

'If you say so, sir,' Kwento replied.

'You don't agree, then?'

'Unfortunately, sir, the Graton planation that Mr Carter referred to is known for growing inferior cotton. You will find that there are far better opportunities elsewhere in America.'

'Oh? And how the hell would you know?'

'I was enslaved in America for six years, sir. I worked on many plantations before arriving here as a stowaway on Captain Walker's ship.'

Strome's tumbler fell to the floor, as he suddenly realised that his hitherto mute slave was speaking to him.

'Well, blow me down,' he exclaimed, sitting bolt upright in his chair. 'You can talk!'

'I can indeed, sir.'

'Wait, so did you come here in disguise or something, or are you just a simple charlatan? Explain yourself.'

'It gave me no pleasure to deceive you, sir. I had good reason for maintaining this charade.'

'I'm listening.'

'Very well,' Kwento let out a deep exhale. 'When I lived in America, I quickly realised that if a black man showed himself to be educated, he would be considered a threat to the planation, and this usually led to him being killed. So, I decided that it would be prudent not to speak, sir.'

'I see,' Strome puffed thoughtfully on his cigar. 'Although that is understandable, I wish that you had been honest with me once you saw that the situation was not the same here.'

'It has become a survival instinct, sir.'

'Very well, but where do we go from here? How do I know that you aren't hiding anything else from me?'

'I could still be of use to you, sir. My wish is to remain in your service, if it pleases you.'

'Hmm, I'm really not sure I could trust you.'

'Please, sir, if you hand me over to the authorities, I'll be sent back to America. That would be a fate worse than death. Besides, I can help you.'

'How could you possibly help me?'

'For one thing, I can point you in the right direction when it comes to trading with the right cotton plantations.'

'Hmm,' Strome lit another cigar. 'Be a good fellow and lock the door, would you.'

He got to his feet and began pacing up and down the room, rubbing his chin as he mulled over everything Kwento had said.

'Sir?' Kwento was confused by the order.

'Just do what I say,' Strome said urgently. 'We have much to discuss.'

Despite his reservations, Kwento locked the door. He had found himself in similar situations with previous masters, and these had invariably not turned out well for him.

'Sit down,' Strome said.

'Why, thank you, sir,' Kwento carefully lowered himself down on the sofa.

'Pour yourself a drink.'

'No, thank you, sir. I do not drink alcohol.'

'Very well. Pray, continue. Tell me everything.'

'It is my humble opinion that Captain Walker and Mr Carter are a pair of twisters, sir.'

'Oh?'

'I have reason to believe that their intention is to cheat you out of your one thousand guineas investment. I know Captain Walker, sir. He is a very cunning man.'

'And what proof do you have to back up these claims?'

'It's like I said earlier, sir. The Graton planation is virtually useless. It's grounds have proven infertile, so much so that the owners were in the process of abandoning it when I was last there.'

'You're certain of this?

'I am, sir.

'Well, what do you propose?

'If you want a good return on your money, I propose that you invest in the Marion plantation in Savanna, Georgia, sir.'

'Then that is what I shall do. I will follow your advice and invest four hundred guineas in this place in Savanna, Georgia, and if it proves a sound decision, a small percentage of the profits shall be yours. How does that sound?'

'That sounds very generous, thank you, sir.'

'Now, may I be so bold as to ask your true identity?'

'My name is Kwento, sir.'

'Is that it, just Kwento?'

'With all due respect, sir, you wouldn't be able to pronounce my full name.'

'Kwento it is, then. Moreover, I will give Bailey the order to remove your neck collar, as an act of good faith as we embark upon this new business partnership.'

'Thank you very much, sir.'

Excited at these most unexpected developments, Strome summoned his wife and daughter to the parlour.

'Colin, what's going on?' Mrs Strome asked nervously. 'Why have you called for us?

'Yes, Daddy, what's this all about?' Miss Sarah added.

'I have a surprise for the both of you. Barthold, if you please,' Strome gestured for Kwento to take the floor.

Against his better judgement, Kwento decided to take revenge on Mrs Strome for the beating she had given him with a fire poker by having a little fun and playing mind games with her, not realising what the consequences of this action would be.

'If I may introduce myself,' he said, speaking loud and clear in his most formal voice, 'my name is Kwento, and I must say that it was so nice to meet Captain Walker again after all this time. The two of you appeared to get on quite well, mistress. Have you known each other long?'

At once, and to his great shock, Mrs Strome dropped to the floor, quickly followed by her daughter, who knelt at her mother's side offering panicked comfort.

'Mummy! Mummy!' she cried. 'Please wake up! Daddy, do something!'

'Don't just stand there,' Strome barked at Kwento. 'Pick her up and put her on the sofa.

Kwento did as he was asked, while Strome rang for Bailey.

'It's OK, Miss Sarah,' Kwento tried to reassure the hysterical girl, 'your mother just has a case of the vapours is all.'

'Get away from her!' Sarah shrieked. 'Haven't you done enough damage, you brute?'

'Oh, calm yourself, Sarah,' Strome said sharply, 'Kwento is only trying to help. Your mother has swooned, that's all. She'll be perfectly alright. Bailey's fetching the salts as we speak.'

'We don't need his help,' Sarah spat. 'He's a turncoat and I hate him!'

'Why would you say that, Miss Sarah?' Kwento asked, wounded by the accusation.

'Because you came here masquerading as someone else. I think that's an accurate definition of a turn coat, don't you?'

'Forgive me, Miss Sarah, but you're mistaking me for a renegade, which I certainly am not. I have already explained everything to your father, and he is happy with my explanation.'

'Yes, Sarah, Kwento is correct,' Strome confirmed. 'Ah, here comes Bailey now.'

The butler immediately administered the smelling salts to Mrs Strome, slowly bringing her around.

'Go on, then,' Sarah continued, 'why the deception? You must think that we are all very stupid, coming here in your sheep's clothing.'

'Miss Sarah, I have–'

'Oh, shut up,' she cut him off. 'I will not speak to the likes of you. Father, kindly remove him from this room.'

'Miss Sarah, please–'

'Perhaps she is right,' Strome mumbled. 'Please return to the kitchen, would you?'

'Of course, sir,' Kwento bowed before leaving the room, followed closely by Bailey.

The pair made their way wordlessly to the kitchen, where Bailey carried out Strome's instruction to remove Kwento's brass neck collar, though not without some difficulty.

'Mr Bailey,' Mrs Alsop gasped in horror, as she and Polly came in through the dining room entrance, 'what are you doing?'

'The master's orders, Mrs Alsop,' Bailey answered, his voice slightly straining with the exertion.

'Well, this is most worrying, Mr Bailey,' Mrs Alsop shook her head. 'Most worrying indeed.'

'Nothing to do with me, Mrs Alsop,' Bailey shrugged, as the rusted lock finally gave way with a loud crack.

'What was all the commotion upstairs?' Polly asked. 'We could hear raised voices and furniture being upset. It nearly made me cry, it did.'

'Oh, shush now, Polly,' Mrs Alsop rolled her eyes. 'Let Mr Bailey talk.'

'All in good time, Mrs Alsop,' Bailey smiled wryly. 'Maybe a cup of nice strong, sweet tea before we start, eh? This could take a little time to explain, I fear.

'Of course, Mr Bailey. Polly, two cups of nice strong, sweet tea, if you please.'

'Can Barthold and me have a cup of nice strong, sweet tea, too?'

'No, you most certainly cannot. Now, if you could bring us up to speed, Mr Bailey?'

'I really don't know where to begin,' Bailey blew out his cheeks. 'Maybe Barthold should be the one to tell it.'

'I'll do my best, Mr Bailey,' Kwento said, as he rubbed at his liberated neck and shoulders.

'Search the Holly book!' Mrs Alsop cried. 'It speaks.'

'Bleeding hell!' Polly yelled, knocking over a saucepan of hot milk and sending it crashing to the floor, along with some of Mrs Alsop's best china.

'Oh, my giddy aunt,' Mrs Alsop threw up her hands. 'I hope you're going to clean that mess up, young madam.'

'Yes, of course,' Polly bowed her head. 'Sorry, Mrs Alsop.'

'Firstly, I must apologise to you all for my deception,' Kwento said. 'I meant no harm by it, I can assure you. Now, please allow me to introduce myself. My name is Kwento.'

'Why did you do it?' Polly cut in.

'Do what?' Kwento asked.

'Why did you deceive me? I thought we were friends.'

'We are friends, Polly.'

'Friends don't lie to each other.

'Polly, come on–'

'Just answer the question,' Mrs Alsop spluttered. 'Why did you do it?'

'Well, the truth is–'

'Just a minute,' Bailey interrupted, 'let me light my pipe first. Hmm, where the hell did I put my tobacco?'

'Oh, just get on with it!' Mrs Alsop was getting exasperated. 'The suspense is killing me!'

'May I continue, Mr Bailey?' Kwento asked.

'Yes,' Bailey nodded. 'Pray, continue.'

'OK, but this may take some time. In order to give you the full picture, I need to go back to the very beginning.'

'Wait, wait,' Polly interjected. 'Shouldn't we bring out some of your delicious homemade macaroons before he begins, Mrs Alsop?'

'Macaroons?' Alsop said. 'You can't have macaroons without a cup of nice strong sweet tea!'

'Exactly,' Polly smirked.

'Search the Holly book! Fine, pour a cup each for you and what's-his-name.'

'His name is Kwento, Mrs Alsop.'

'Oh, shut up and fetch my delicious homemade macaroons while you're at it.'

'Yes, Mrs Alsop.'

'Now, can we please get on with the story.'

'Very well,' Kwento nodded. 'Six years ago, whilst out on manoeuvres with my lieutenant, I was suddenly ambushed and attacked by the Arab slaver Mustafa and his band of mercenaries. I fought for my life, wrestling each one to the ground like a wild bear, but in the end, the odds were simply too great, and they were able to overpower and then spirit me away from my homeland.'

'Are you saying that you were once a soldier?' Bailey asked.

'My rank was that of a young warrior, which is perhaps similar to a cadet, going by Anglo-American standards. Anyway, it turned out I had been set up by my own lieutenant, who had traded me in for a baker rifle.'

'How awful,' Polly frowned.

The reason why Kwento was not being honest in his account of what happened when he was captured back in Africa was quite simple: he was embarrassed by the truth. He wasn't a brave warrior back then; he was just a terrified little boy.

'Be quiet, Polly,' Mrs Alsop said. 'Let him speak.'

'I was manacled and placed in a narrow boat,' Kwento continued, 'before being taken on a very long journey down the coast to Senegal, where I was put onboard a large ship. Can you

Imagine how I felt, knowing that I would never see my mother or my homeland ever again?'

A feeling of great shame fell upon those assembled in the kitchen, as Kwento began to enjoy being the centre of attention, and started playing to his rapt audience.

'You know, I must say, Mrs Alsop, these macaroons are simply delicious,' he said, taking a deliberate pause.

'That's why I call them my delicious homemade macaroons, Mr Kwento,' Mrs Alsop replied, puffing her chest out with pride.

This drew a sideways glance from Polly, who smiled upon realising that for the first time, Mrs Alsop had actually addressed Kwento as though he was a human being, and not merely a possession.

Perhaps he does have voodoo magic after all, she thought.

'Ahem,' Bailey forced a cough. 'Pray, continue.'

'Of course, please forgive me,' Kwento laughed, wiping the crumbs away from his mouth. 'My tastebuds distracted me for a moment.'

'That's quite alright, Mr Kwento,' Mrs Alsop beamed. 'Here, have another of my delicious homemade macaroons.'

'Why, thank you, Mrs Alsop.'

'Can we please get on with it?' Bailey said, getting frustrated himself now.'

'Well, from Senegal, I was taken on a long, hazardous voyage across the sea to New Orleans, and then on to Savanna, Georgia via Mobile, Alabama, where I was put to work on a cotton plantation along with a hundred other slaves. The work was back-breaking, and our treatment was often brutal. I can still hear the masters whip to this day.'

Kwento had deliberately skipped over the story of his hazardous voyage because he thought the details would be far too graphic for the ears around the table, and also because he didn't want to remember what he had tried so hard to forget. He then appeared to drift off momentarily, as though lost in his memories, only to be quickly pulled back to the here and now by Polly's direct line of questioning.

'Well, why didn't you leave?' she asked. 'Couldn't you have just run away?'

'Oh, my dear Polly,' he laughed bitterly, 'you just don't understand. I was shackled there, just like I was here.'

'Yes, well, we can now see how that was wrong,' Mrs Alsop said, clearly embarrassed. 'We've released you now, though, and that's all that matters.'

'Indeed, Mrs Alsop,' Kwento allowed.

'Let the lad finish, Mrs Alsop,' Bailey pleaded.

'After spending three years in Savanna, I was taken to another cotton plantation near Knoxville, Tennessee,' Kwento went on, 'and then finally, after a year there, I was transferred to a small tobacco planation in Richmond, Virginia which only had twenty slaves, and that's where I was taught to read and write by the master.'

'And how to speak English,' Polly added.

'Actually, I could already speak English.'

'So, how did you end up here?' Bailey asked.

'I was helped by a free slave named Edward Smith.'

'Wait, are you saying that there were free slaves walking around the plantation?'

'Yes, some even worked as overseers for the master, as did some of the more trusted slaves.'

'Let me get this straight. You're saying that ex-slaves were brought in to supervise the slaves still in captivity, is that it?'

'Well, not exactly "brought in," no. Usually, they were from the same plantation, but had somehow managed to buy their own freedom from the master.'

'This is most extraordinary,' Bailey shook his head in disbelief.'

Tell us how you escaped, Mr Kwento,' Mrs Alsop said.

'Yes, um, where was I?'

'Search the Holly book! You were talking about the free slave, Edward Smith.'

Yes, of course. So, Edward was involved with the Vigilance Committee, which is based in Philadelphia.'

'Who are they?' Polly asked.

'Will you shut up and stop interrupting, Polly,' Mrs Alsop shouted. 'Don't open your mouth on matters that you don't fully understand, girl.'

'You don't understand, either, Mrs Alsop,' Polly retorted. 'Otherwise, you wouldn't keep asking questions yourself.'

'I've just about had enough of your lip, young miss,' Mrs Alsop became incensed, jumping to her feet, her face flushed red. 'Get out of here! Go on, clear off!'

Polly got up to leave, but as she looked around the table with tears welling in her eyes, Kwento felt compelled to intervene.

'No, please let her stay, Mrs Alsop,' he said. 'She needs to hear this. Besides, she may even learn something.'

'Pffft, her, learn something?' Mrs Alsop sniggered. 'I very much doubt it. She's as thick as that brass saucepan on the stove that one.'

'I'm more than sure that there will be no more interruptions if you allow her to stay,' Bailey said. 'Isn't that right, Polly?'

'Yes, Mr Bailey,' Polly whispered.

A huffing Mrs Alsop retook her seat, saying nothing.

'Please continue,' Bailey turned to Kwento.

'The Vigilance Committee is a group of Quakers – abolitionists – who have vowed to end slavery. Edward Smith was one of their earliest successes, and after deciding that he was going to help me, he arranged for me to board a small vessel that was moored at Hampton Harbour in Virginia. From there, I was taken to New York, where I stowed away on Captain Walker's ship, the Merry, which just so happened to be bound for Liverpool.'

'How long did it take you to get here?' Mrs Alsop asked.

'About six weeks.'

'Six weeks! Search the Holly book!'

'I actually consider that a short journey, compared to the voyage from Africa to the Americas.'

'Six weeks? Short?'

'At sea, absolutely. Normally, you could expect to be out there for at least three months, depending on which passage you take.'

'How did you survive?' Bailey quizzed. 'I mean, if you were a stowaway, what did you do for food and drink?'

'I was discovered not long after we set sail, and luckily enough, they decided not to throw me overboard. I lived and ate with the crew.'

'Were there other slaves on board?' Mrs Alsop asked.

'No, slaves are usually taken to America. They only ever leave in their presence of their masters. The Merry was transporting sugar, tobacco and barley, not slaves. Anyway, when we eventually arrived at the Coburg Dock in Liverpool, Captain Walker handed me over to the authorities, who placed me outside a coffee house. That's where I was auctioned off and bought by Mr Strome.'

Well, that was a very interesting story, Mr Kwento, and thank you for sharing it with us,' Mrs Alsop said. 'More tea anyone?'

Bailey rose up from his chair and walked over to the old Welsh dresser. Pulling out the draw, he took hold of a large leather-bound book, which he brought back to the dining table and sat down.

'The master instructed me to teach you quotes from the good book,' he said to Kwento, opening the book and turning the first page. 'Now that I know you can speak the King's, I think this would be a good time to start over.'

'Yes,' Kwento said, 'but–'

No buts,' Bailey cut him off. 'These are the master's wishes and I must obey, understand?'

'Yes, Mr Bailey, it's just–'

'We will begin at the very first passage,' Bailey attached a tiny pair of spectacles to the end of his nose. 'Now, it came to pass that after Alexander, the son of Philip the Macedonian, who first reigned in Greece, coming out of the land of Cethim, had overthrown Darius, king of the Persians and Medes–'

'And he fought many battles,' Kwento interrupted, 'and took the strongholds of all, and slew the kings of the earth.'

There was a stunned silence around the table, which was eventually broken by a gobsmacked Bailey.'

'Good lord,' he said, 'how do you know that?'

'As I was trying to tell you, Mr Bailey,' Kwento smiled, 'I was baptised and converted to Christianity by the missionaries in Nigeria back in 1820.'

Before Bailey could say another word, there was a loud knocking at the tradesmen's door.

'There's a young gentleman and lady here to see you, Mrs Alsop,' Polly announced.

'Hello Mum,' the visitor said.

'Oh, my dear lord!' Mrs Alsop cried at the top of her voice, before raising her hands to her face and beginning to weep. 'Mr Bailey, this is my son Michael.'

'Very pleased to meet you, Michael,' Bailey extended his hand.

'Likewise, Mr Bailey,' Michael accepted Bailey's hand. 'And may I introduce my fiancée, Myfanwy.'

'Myfanny!' Mrs Alsop gasped. 'What sort of a name is that for a young lady?'

'I think you'll find that it's pronounced muh-van-wi, Mrs Alsop,' Bailey smirked.

'It's a Welsh name, Mother,' Michael coughed. 'Myfanwy is from the Rhondda Valley.'

'It's very nice to meet you, Mrs Alsop,' Myfanwy nodded.

'My, you're a big lass, aren't you?'

'Mother, please!' Michael's face reddened.

'I know someone who's Welsh,' Polly chimed in.

'No, you don't,' Mrs Alsop snapped. 'Shut up, Polly.'

'But I do know someone who's Welsh, Mrs Alsop.'

'Always got to be involved somehow, don't you?

'Do you really know a Welsh person, Polly?' Mr Bailey asked.

'Mrs Jones,' Polly answered. She lives next door to my mam and dad.'

'And do you know which part of Wales Mrs Jones is from?'

'Um,' Polly thought for a while. 'Not sure really, no.'

'And you wonder why I keep losing my temper with her,' Mrs Alsop said. 'The girl is a complete fantasist.'

'But it's true, Mrs Alsop,' Polly protested. 'I do know Mrs Jones. She even talks funny, just like Miss Myfanwy… Sorry, Miss Myfanwy. I didn't mean anything by that.'

'Oh, that's quite alright, Polly,' Myfanwy laughed. 'I get that every where I go.'

The mines in the Rhondda Valley provided work for most of the people who lived in the area, save for the farmers who toiled across the vast landscape. Myfanwy's father and three brothers all worked in the mining industry, and between them had paid for her education. She was very grateful for the sacrifices her family had made on her behalf, for she was under no illusions when it came to the dangers that lurked deep beneath the wet Welsh soil. Her first love, a Mr Berwyn Roberts, had been killed instantly in a freak mining accident two years prior, leaving Myfanwy totally devastated and depressed, to the point where her mother became convinced that she would never recover from the trauma. Then, suddenly, and seemingly out of nowhere, Myfanwy announced her engagement to Michael Alsop. This rocked her parents to the core, it being inconceivable to them that she would deliberately put herself in the same position once again by marrying a coal miner.

'Oh, where are my manners?' Bailey chuckled. 'Please, come join us at the table.'

'Thank you, Mr Bailey,' Michael said, as he and Myfanwy took their places at the table.

The couple smiled politely, all the while stealing furtive glances at Polly and Kwento.

'This is Polly, the scullery maid,' Bailey said, taking on the role of host, 'and the dark gentleman is Kwento, the house boy.'

Michael and Myfanwy exchanged somewhat bemused looks, but nodded respectfully anyway.

'Pleased to meet you, Kwento,' Michael said.

'Likewise, Master Michael,' Kwento replied. 'Please forgive my curiosity, Master Michael, but what is Wales?'

Michael turned to Myfanwy, and they both started laughing loudly, as did everyone else sitting around the table, but Kwento didn't get the joke.

'Wales is a country,' Michael answered, wiping a tear from his eye.

'Myfanwy and I live in South Wales, in a place called the Rhondda Valley, about one hundred and sixty miles from here.'

'Ah, now I understand,' Kwento said. 'Thank you, Master Michael. So, it must have been quite a long journey for you both?'

'It wasn't too bad, actually.'

'Well,' Mrs Alsop piped up at last. 'This is a surprise, isn't it, Mr Bailey?'

'Indeed it is, Mrs Alsop,' Bailey agreed. 'Your mother speaks of you often, Michael.'

Michael smiled at this, despite knowing it to be a lie, having seen the look of surprise on Bailey's face when he and Myfanwy were first introduced. It didn't bother him, though. He knew that his mother was a proud and private person, so much so that he still didn't know the reason why his parents had separated. As far as he knew, it just happened, and nothing more was ever said about it. His mother had always maintained a hard outer shell and never wore her heart on her sleeve, but he knew that deep down inside, she had a heart of gold, even if she chose not to show it.

He had been just five years old when his parents separated, and he was sent to live with his grandmother Ginny, who he loved very dearly. In fact, it was Grandma Ginny who persuaded his mother to leave him with her and enter into service. By volunteering to help look after baby Michael, Ginny was fulfilling what she thought was a debt to Mary, having taken her out of school to help wash clothes for a living as she, too, was a single parent at the time. This meant that Mary missed out on an education, leaving her with no choice but to go into service. Then, at age fourteen, Michael followed in his father's footsteps and went into mining, first as a waggoner in Bold Colliery, Lancashire, before moving to and settled down in the Rhondda Valley, where he worked as a tunneller.

'All good, I hope, Mr Bailey?' he smiled broadly.

'Of course,' Bailey winked. 'Polly, pour Michael and Myfanwy a nice strong, sweet cup of tea, would you?'

'Shall I fetch a plate of Mrs Alsop's delicious homemade macaroons as well?' Polly asked.

'Yes, why not,' Mrs Alsop said. 'This is, after all, a special occasion. Oh, and put a few extra macaroons on the plate for Myfanwy. I can see she likes her food.'

'Mother, please!'

'Well, I must say that it's very nice to see you after all this time, Michael.'

'I know it's been a while, Mother, but I've sent plenty of letters.

'True enough, but it's not the same as actually seeing someone in the flesh, is it?'

'I promise not to leave it so long next time.'

'How long are you here for anyway?'

'Two days. Myfanwy wanted to visit Liverpool.'

'Yes, I wanted to see where your son grew up, Mrs Alsop. He's told me so much about the town.'

'Indeed, and may I ask where you're staying?'

'We're staying at lodgings, Mrs Alsop,' Myfanwy said. 'In a place called Upper Pitt Street, I believe.'

'Upper Pitt Street! Is that right, Michael?'

'Yes, why?'

'Because Upper Pitt Street's full of Chinese, that's why!'

'That doesn't bother me, Mother,' Michael shrugged. 'I don't have a problem with the other races.'

'Ahem,' Mrs Alsop sniffed, feeling Kwento's eyes on her, 'neither do I.'

'I work with people from all over the place down the mines,'

Michael continued. 'Down there, we're all the same. What's your story, Kwento?'

'Pardon?'

'You're from Africa, I take it?'

'I am, yes.'

'So, how did you come to find yourself here in Liverpool?'

'Unfortunately, I was ensnared by the slave trade triangle.

'Ah yes, I've heard of this, but I don't know much about it. Why is it called a triangle?'

'It's a general term that is used to describe the three main slave shipping routes between Europe, Africa and the Americas.'

'Really? I'd always thought of slavery as a strictly American enterprise.'

'Not quite. The British got involved as far back as the sixteenth century, but it began long before that with the Portuguese and the Spanish. The triangle runs from Great Britain to the Congo in West Africa, and then across to Brazil and up to the Caribbean en route to North America.'

'And how did you come to be caught up in all this?'

'I was kidnapped from my home in Nigeria, and then taken by force to America, where I stayed for six years until I managed to escape to New York. From there, I stowed away onboard a British ship, which brought me here to England.'

'I can't even begin to imagine what that must have been like for you,' Michael shook his head. 'I am truly sorry.'

'It's not your fault, Master Michael. The blame lies with the greedy merchants and government officials who have made vast fortunes on the back of human suffering.'

While Michael and Kwento were talking, Mrs Alsop leaned in close to Bailey and whispered in his ear, asking him to change the subject. She had already heard Kwento relate his sad story, and was now becoming uncomfortable with the awkward topic of slavery.

'I seem to remember Mrs Alsop telling me that you followed in your father's footsteps as a miner,' Bailey said. 'Is that correct, Michael?'

'Yes, that is correct, Mr Bailey,' Michael said. 'I first went down the mines when I was fourteen years old.'

'That must have been very frightening for a young boy?'

'It certainly was at first, but I wasn't the only youngster. There were quite a few of us, so we sort of stuck together.'

'Myfanwy, please tell us all how you and our Michael first met,' Mrs Alsop said. 'More tea anyone?'

'Well, it's quite a tragic story, but one with a happy ending, I'm glad to say,' Myfanwy smiled sheepishly. 'I first met Michael eight months ago, when I was in hospital.'

'Oh, you poor girl. What was wrong with you?

'There was nothing wrong with her, Mother,' Michael said. 'I was the patient.'

'I don't understand.'

'I had an accident, and Myfanwy helped nurse me back to health.'

'Oh, so you're a nurse, Myfanwy?'

'Yes, Mrs Alsop.'

'I see. Why were you in hospital, Michael, and why didn't you think to tell me?'

'I was hurt down the mine, and I didn't tell you because I didn't want you worrying about me.'

'Search the Holly book! Didn't want me worrying?'

'It was nothing serious, Mother.'

'I don't know about that,' Myfanwy said. 'You did almost drown.'

'Almost drowned!' Mrs Alsop exclaimed. 'Michael, what's she talking about?'

'We had a small cave-in, that's all,' Michael said. 'It happens all the time, Mother. It was nothing, honestly.'

'I'll be the judge of that.'

'Mother, please don't go on.'

'Myfanwy, what happened? I want the truth of it.'

'Well, there was a massive cave-in at the pit.'

'Massive!' Alsop gasped, as Michael shot Myfanwy a glare.

'Yes, it trapped at least twenty men, including your son, as water started to pour into the shaft, filling it quickly.'

Mrs Alsop put her head in her hands and let out a muffled moan of emotion, as Bailey leaned across to comfort her.

'There, there, Mrs Alsop,' he put an arm around her shoulder, 'don't you go upsetting yourself. Michael's here now, safe and well.'

'That's not the point,' she looked up with watery eyes. 'It's the fact that he didn't even bother to tell me. How could you, Michael?'

'Really, Mother, it was nothing,' Michael repeated.

'If it was nothing, what were you doing in hospital?'

'I swallowed a bit of water, that's all.'

'Myfanwy said that you nearly drowned. Sounds like more than a bit of water to me.'

Michael had good reason to play down what had happened, knowing that the truth would have been far too distressing for his mother to bear. The collapse had crushed six miners under the weight of the coal, and then a further eight miners were drowned shortly after, leaving only six survivors, himself included. His memory of the incident was blurry to say the least, but he had somehow managed to swim through the thick black slurry and found a pocket of air trapped in the recess above, before swimming back and pulling the other five survivors up into the pocket with him. The space they were in was cramped and hot, and the men had to paddle desperately for six hours in total darkness to keep their heads above the water line until they were finally rescued. By then, the air had become stale, and all were in a state of exhaustion and nearing death when they finally arrived at the hospital. The other five all retired due to poor health, but once Michael had made a full recovery, he was promoted to the job of banksman, which guaranteed that he would never have to go back underground again. He also received a medal for bravery from the Dinas Ishaf mining company, for his heroic actions in saving the lives of his five fellow miners.

'How about another cup of tea?' Bailey suggested.

'Are you two engaged, Master Michael?' Polly asked.

'Yes, we are, Polly,' Michael said, raising Myfanwy's hand to show off the braided gold ring. 'And we intend to be married soon.'

'Oh, look at that ring, Mrs Alsop,' Polly gushed. 'It's absolutely gorgeous.'

'Gorgeous indeed,' Mrs Alsop huffed, 'but you'll get married over my dead body! I mean, no offence to you, Myfanwy, but you hardly know our Michael.'

'Oh, come off it, Mother,' Michael laughed. 'We love each other very much, and I can't think of anyone else I would rather spend the rest of my life with.'

'Ah, young love, Mrs Alsop,' Bailey beamed. "Where you not impetuous before you were married?'

'Certainly not, Mr Bailey,' Mrs Alsop spluttered. 'We courted for at least a year before we even considered getting married, and it still ended up a bloody disaster!'

'Just because you had a bad marriage doesn't mean that we will,

Mother,' Michael said.

'Your father was a bloody waste of time.'

'Well, I'm glad you brought him up, Mother.'

'Really? Why?'

'There are two reasons why I came to see you today. One was to introduce you to Myfanwy, and the other was to tell you that my father, your husband, is dying.'

'What do you mean, he's dying? Your father's as strong as an ox.'

'The doctor says he has black lung, Mother. Too many years down the mines, I'm afraid.'

'Dear, dear. How long has he got?'

'A couple of weeks, maybe months at best.'

'I'm sorry to hear that, Michael. Truly, I am.'

'Thank you, Mother. Anyway, I think it's time we were going.'

'What? So soon! You've only just got here.'

'I know, but we've only got two days, and half of this one is gone already.'

'I understand, but don't leave it so long next time. You know where I am.'

'I will see you soon, Mother,' Michael stood. 'Well, it was really nice to meet you all, Mr Bailey, Polly, Kwento.'

Handshakes and well-wishes were exchanged, and then Michael hugged his mother before leaving the same way that he and Myfanwy had entered, through the tradesmen's entrance.

CARDS ON THE TABLE

In the front parlour, Mrs Strome was laying splayed out across the floral-patterned sofa, still recovering from her fainting episode, while being attended to by her daughter.

'Mummy, we need to get rid of the African,' Sarah said.

'You've changed your tune,' Mrs Strome raised an eyebrow. 'I thought you were his champion. I thought he'd worked his juju magic on you.'

'I was never beguiled by him, Mummy.'

Mrs Strome was immediately suspicious of her daughter's quick turnaround regarding the slave, but while her instincts told her that something was not quite adding up, she couldn't put her finger on what it was just yet.

'Well, if not voodoo then what other hold could he possibly have had over you?' she probed. 'When he first arrived here, you were strutting around like the Queen of Sheba, and now look at you, plotting his demise.'

'I can assure you that the African has no hold over me,' Sarah insisted. 'How could you even think a thing like that, Mummy?'

'I just find it strange how quickly you've gone from stroking his nappy head to wanting him gone from the very place you so vigorously campaigned to keep him.'

'I just want him gone. I don't feel safe with him around.'

'I want to know why. I can't help you if you won't tell me.

'Very well,' Sarah sighed. 'The slave and I are lovers, and have been so ever since he entered this house.'

Mrs Strome burst into laughter as she reached for a handkerchief to wipe her eyes, but then, to her horror, she realised that her daughter was not laughing along with her.

'You are joking, aren't you?' she asked, her voice quivering with desperation.'

'We were an item,' Sarah answered, 'but now we are not.'

'What do you mean, "an item?" Are you telling me you have slept with him?'

'Many times, yes.'

'What!'

'It wasn't always just about intercourse, though. We sometimes just cuddled.'

'Just cuddled! Listen to yourself, you stupid little bitch! I don't know what to say, I really don't.'

'What does it matter? It's over now anyway.'

'Oh, just shut up and let me think,' Mrs Strome turned away in disgust. ' I will have to speak with your father.'

'What are you going to tell him?'

'I haven't decided yet. Just get out of my sight, you rotten little trollop.'

' Yes, Mummy.'

Sarah stepped out into the hallway wearing a smug look on her face, only for her heart to skip a beat when he mother called her back into the parlour.

'Yes, Mummy?' she said timidly.

'I shall ask you once again, are you sure you want him gone?'

'Yes, Mummy.'

'Then leave me. I have business to attend to.'

'Yes, Mummy.'

Mrs Strome was sitting on the chesterfield in the morning, reading a book, while Mr Strome read the newspaper in his easy chair.

'Colin?'

'Yes, dear?'

'We need to talk.'

'About what, dear?'

'The African. We need to talk about the African.'

Strome sighed as he folded his paper and removed his small reading glasses.

'Kwento?' he said. 'What about him?'

'Sarah wants him out of the house, and quite frankly, so do I.'

Strome unfolded his paper and buried his head in it.

'You know, it says here that Admiral Codrington is to receive the Grand Cross of the Bath from King George himself,' he said, 'for his victory in the battle of Navarino.

'Colin?'

'Doesn't your cousin Barnaby know Admiral Codrington?'

'Yes, and he says Codrington only won the battle by being a bully and ignoring orders. The man is a complete arse by all accounts.'

'Good lord, listen to this. A fifteen-year-old girl was kidnapped from a Liverpool boarding school. It says here–'

'Colin?'

'Ellen Turner was collected by Mr Edward Wakefield's servant, a Mr Thevenot, who was masquerading as her ward, but Mistress Margaret Daulby became suspicious when Ellen did not seem to recognise the man, and informed the authorities immediately.'

'Colin?'

'Just a moment, dear. Ellen was taken to Manchester, where she was introduced to thirty-year-old Edward Wakefield, who then took her to Gretna Green and married her, before fleeing to Calais. Well, I'll be blown.'

'Colin?'

'Mr Turner, father of Ellen, sent a police detective and Solicitor to France, and Mr Wakefield was eventually arrested and brought back to England, where he was tried and found guilty by a Lancaster jury, and sentenced to three years imprisonment at Newgate.'

'Colin!'

'Yes, dear?'

'The African must go.'

'I'm afraid he's become too useful to me, my dear. We can make a lot of money off his knowledge, so I suggest you get to know him a little better. Be a bit nicer to him, and believe me, your kindness will pay dividends.'

'Of course, this new partnership the two of you have struck up. Have you any idea how ridiculous that sounds? My husband, advised by a slave.'

'Well, I have to tell you that the investment he recommended looks like making us quite a lot of money. Kwento seems to be a man of his word, just remember that.'

'Very well. I shall try and get along with the brute, but I can assure you that it won't be easy.'

The staff had retired for the night, with only Polly and Kwento remaining in the kitchen. Polly was clearing things away, and Kwento was standing in the doorway of the scullery, watching.

'Polly, why won't you talk to me?' he asked.

'I've been told I'm to keep away from you, so please leave me alone.'

'But there's so much I have to say to you. Please talk to me, Polly. There's nobody else here. What harm could it do?'

'I nearly lost my job because of you, so no, I will not talk to you.'

'Sweet Polly, you do know that I have feelings for you, don't you?

'Frankly, I don't care, thank you very much.

'I've loved you from the moment I first saw you, Polly, and I know you have the same feelings for me. I could hear it in your voice when you used to sit here in this scullery late at night and talk the hours away.'

'I did have feelings for you, that is true, but it was before I knew you had lied to me.'

'Oh, Polly, don't have me raked over the old coals again, as you English would say. I've explained everything. What more would you have me do?'

'Mrs Alsop was right about you. You're nothing but trouble.'

'What does Mrs Alsop know? She's had it in for me right from the very beginning. Please, Polly, come and sit with me. I won't keep you long, I promise.'

Polly thought for a moment before taking a step towards the scullery, but she would go no further than the threshold of the doorway.

'What is it that you want to say to me?' she asked. 'Make it quick, because I've lots of work to do.'

'Well, first of all, I've noticed that you don't speak the same as the others in the house. Why is that?'

'What do you mean?'

'Your voice sounds different than Mrs Alsop's or Mr Bailey's.'

'Oh, it's just because I'm Irish.'

'Irish? Is that your tribe?'

'Oh, you're so funny, Kwento,' she giggled. 'Don't you know anything about Ireland?'

'I'm afraid not, although I do remember hearing others speak like you do when I was in America.'

'Ireland is a country, like Wales. It's just across the water from here.'

'Ah, so you're from the other side of the River Mersey, correct?'

'No, that's somewhere else. Look, I'm not bright enough to explain it all to you properly.'

'Dearest Polly, you mustn't put yourself down like that. You're the brightest person I've ever known. You stand out from all the others.'

'Oh? Then why does Mrs Alsop say that I'm as thick as a saucepan?'

'Polly, listen to me. You're brighter than they are because you always speak truthfully. You speak from the heart, and you always say what you see and mean what you say, and that's why I love you so much.'

'If you loved me so much, you would never have let Miss Sarah into your bed.'

'How did you know about that?'

Kwento was so shocked and embarrassed by Polly's revelation that he didn't really know what else to say to her, and instead simply lowered his head in shame.

'I know everything that goes on in this house,' she said. 'Nothing gets past me.'

'If that is true, you will also know that Miss Sarah forced herself upon me.'

Polly had hitherto kept secret the fact that when Miss Sarah chased her away and barred the scullery door from the inside, Polly had re-entered the kitchen and listened to everything that happened.

'Oh, and I suppose you really didn't enjoy it?' she asked pointedly. 'You could have said no.'

'How could I say no, Polly? If the master forced himself upon you, would you be able to refuse?'

'I suppose not,' Polly's said quietly, after a moment's consideration.

Kwento approached Polly and, after seeing that she did not move away, took her in his arms and held her close, brushing aside her thick, red wavy hair with the back of his hand as he looked deep into her pale blue eyes.

'You've got to listen to me,' he said. 'To them upstairs, we're nothing more than property, to be used as they see fit, and then discarded like old rubbish once we're not useful anymore. It's you that I love, Polly, not Miss Sarah. You must believe me.'

'I don't know what to believe anymore,' she sighed. 'Part of me wants to believe you, but I'm confused.'

He led her over to his cot. Polly removed her apron, and they sat quietly for a moment before he slowly brought his face closer to hers until they became engaged in a long, lingering kiss.

'Please give me a second chance, Polly,' he begged. 'I would never do anything to hurt you, you must believe me.'

'Oh, you could charm the birds right out of the trees, you could,' she laughed, cuddling up to him. 'Anyway, enough about my accent. What did you really want to talk to me about?'

'See, I told you that you're bright,' he smiled. 'You've seen right through me. OK now, listen. I have a plan that will get us both out of here, Polly, and if it works, you'll never have to worry about money or anything else ever again.' He pulled her in close and began to whisper. 'I've become a personal advisor to the master.

'And what's that supposed to mean?'

'It means that I tell the master where to buy the best cotton in America, and every time he makes a profit, I get a bonus. We're going to be rich, Polly. Rich beyond our wildest dreams, don't you understand?'

'Um, not really.'

'That's alright, it will all become clear in time. Now, listen very carefully to what I'm about to say. The master has already given me an advance payment of ten guineas, and there's more on the way.'

'Ten guineas! Bleeding hell.'

'Shush! Keep your voice down. I've hidden it behind one of the bricks here in the scullery wall.

'So, the master pays you for information?'

'Yes, and when I have enough money, my intention is to get us the hell out of here. We're going to leave this place, Polly, just me and you.'

'But where would we go?'

'Well, when I was travelling to Liverpool on the Merry, I overheard a crewman talking about buying a small croft with land somewhere on the outskirts of the town. Could you see yourself as a farmer's wife?'

'Oh, Kwento,' Polly began to weep. 'Please tell me this isn't a joke. Could it really be true?'

'Believe it, Polly. This will happen, but we must be patient. It may take a little time to gather enough money for what we need.'

Kwento was in a better place now that he was with Polly, and there was no more secrecy or playing the dumb mute. It felt good to finally be able to communicate with her properly, and to talk to each other like normal human beings. Ever since they had first met back in the dark, old grey kitchen, it had seemed inevitable that this moment would come, and as they embraced again, she kissed him passionately as he lowered her down gently onto his narrow cot. Slowly, he began to unbutton her crisp white blouse, staring lovingly into her large, round, innocent blue eyes.'

'I really do love you, Polly,' he whispered, before pressing down hard, forcing her to wince slightly as she held his muscular shoulders with both hands.

The experience they shared was completely different to what he had known with Miss Sarah. It was gentle, more relaxed and more loving, and it was in this very moment that he realised that Polly was pure and unspoilt. He pressed down upon her again, eliciting a faint sigh as their bodies tightened. He caressed her pale white neck with his lips, and ran his fingers slowly and carefully across her soft bare breasts, following the natural curve of her arm stopping at her hand, before pressing down one last time, as their joining ended as quickly and passionately as it had begun.

Mrs Strome was in the morning room when there came a light knocking at the door, before Kwento entered dressed in his finery. He wore a smart red tailored waistcoat, with tight white trousers, long white socks and shiny black shoes.

'You wanted to see me, madam?' he said.

'Ah yes,' Mrs Strome gestured towards a chair opposite, 'please take a seat.'

'I'd rather stand, if it's all the same to you, madam.'

'I said sit down!'

'If you insist, madam.'

'Yes, I do insist. This is going to be very difficult,' she mumbled under her breath. 'I believe we might have got off on the wrong foot, so to speak.'

'The wrong foot, madam?'

'Don't get cute with me. You know exactly what I'm talking about.'

'Yes, you're referring to the time you decided to beat me half senseless with a fire poker, madam.'

'Good, we're on the same page.'

'Indeed, madam.'

Polly then entered through the open door, carrying a large silver tray with a pot of tea, two cups and saucers, a small jug of milk and a small bowl of sugar balanced precariously.

'Just leave the tray on the table, Polly,' Mrs Strome said. 'I'll serve myself, thank you. You may go.'

Polly and Kwento exchanged glances, both recognising that the lady was acting suspiciously out of character.

'Well, go on, you silly cow,' Mrs Strome waved her off, 'away with you.'

'Yes, mistress,' Polly left with a bow, stopping in the doorway to shoot Kwento a concerned look.'

'You shouldn't have spoken to Polly like that, madam,' Kwento said. 'I think you were very rude.'

'I shall speak to her as I please,' Mrs Strome sneered. 'Kindly keep your opinions to yourself. Anyway, where were we?'

'I believe you were about to apologise, madam,' Kwento suggested.

'Remember your place here, slave,' she said darkly.

'Forgive me, madam,' he allowed himself a wry smile. 'I meant no disrespect.'

'Look, it's no secret that you and I are never going to be friends, but for the sake of my husband's business, I've accepted that I must find a way to put up with you… milk?'

'I take mine black, madam.'

'Of course,' she forced a smile as she began to pour, but this was soon wiped from her face when Kwento spoke again.

'Will Captain Walker be visiting with us again soon, madam? I did so enjoy seeing him again.'

Her face contorted with rage, Mrs Strome marched over to the fireplace and picked up the dreaded poker. This prompted Kwento to jump to his feet in alarm, as she backed him up against the wall with the tip of the poker held menacingly under his chin. She moved in so near that he could feel the warmth of her peppermint breath on his face, and smell the sweet scent of her clean, shiny auburn hair. He had never had cause to study her features this closely before, and he could not help but acknowledge that there was a strange beauty about her.

'I must warn you, Mrs Strome, that if you hurt me again, I will reveal the secret plan that you and Captain Walker have hatched to murder your husband.'

The lady's anger ebbed away as quickly as it had surfaced, and her warm olive complexion soon returned. Her dark hazel-brown eyes seemed to be penetrating his very soul as she stared at him deeply with a half-smile, moving in closer and closer. Her nostrils flared and her bottom lip began to quiver. She was now so close that he could hear the beating of her heart deep within her heaving bosom, and instinct told him to brace himself for something unexpected that was about to happen. Then, she leaned forward and, with a soft low growl, pressed her thin red lips up against his, as she gently cradled the back of his head in her slender hand, only for him to turn his head to the side.

She stepped back with a perplexed look on her face, and then almost immediately regained her composure. No man had ever been able to resist her womanly wiles before,. .

Is this a ploy to buy my silence regarding Walker's plot to murder her husband ? he wondered.

Whatever the reason, she now looked absolutely furious at having been rejected.

'I never should have listened to my husband,' she said. 'I knew this was a mistake. You think you're quite the fucking man, don't you, trying to blackmail me?'

'On the contrary, Agnes. I know I am a slave.'

'I'm getting sick and tired of your insolent talk. Who the hell do you think you are? It's mistress or Mrs Strome when you address me, understand?'

'Yes, Agnes.'

'By the way, I know you've been sleeping with Sarah,' Mrs Strome said, scanning his face for a reaction. 'What, cat got your tongue?'

'I've no idea what you're talking about.'

'Oh, don't play dumb with me. She has already confessed the truth of the whole sordid affair.'

'Very well, I admit it is true,' he sighed, 'but know this. It was your daughter who forced herself upon me – many times, I might add.'

'Just get out,' she spat. 'You disgust me!'

The altercation left her feeling restless and agitated.

How dare he spurn my advances, she thought bitterly, as she went over to the writing bureau and took out a piece of paper before sitting down and beginning to write:

My dearest James,

I'm writing to you in deep despair. The slave has announced

that he can speak in perfect English, and has introduced himself as Kwento. I need not explain to you the seriousness of this revelation, and advise that you turn your attention to this most pressing matter, and deal with the other at a later date. I trust that you will execute a new plan as quickly as possible.

I am yours,

Agnes.

POLLY SPEAKS UP

The business partnership that Kwento had entered into with Colin Strome appeared to be a very profitable one, with the former accruing quite a lot of money to stash secretly within the cold, damp wall of the scullery. At the rate things were going, it would not be long before he reached his goal of having enough money for Polly and himself to retire from service and set up a farming business of their own. Strome had, on Kwento's advice, recently invested a further fifteen thousand guineas into a fertile cotton plantation somewhere outside Knoxville, Tennessee, and the early signs were looking good, but little did either man know that a storm was headed in their direction at a rate of knots.

In Sefton Park, in the Toxteth area of Liverpool, Mrs Strome and Captain James Walker were walking arm-in-arm along the wide footpath that ran alongside the old boating lake. The sun was shining brightly, as they mingled amongst the many other courting couples that were strolling about in the fresh open air, though Mrs Strome still took the precaution of matching a large hat, complete with a veil, with her pale-blue dress.'Captain Walker wore a tight fitting dark grey suit with matching bowler hat and black shiny leather shoes.

'It feels like everyone's watching us, James,' she said, speaking in a hushed voice not realising that it was only the guilt in her pretty head playing tricks on her.

'It's just your imagination, my dear,' he dismissed her concerns. 'Everyone is far too busy with their own business to notice anyone else's.'

'Oh, I do love coming here, you know. Being out in the fresh air, it's so invigorating, don't you think?'

'Yes, and as a mariner, I do feel more at home when close to water,' he gestured toward the lake. 'Even a body as small as this.'

'If you love being at sea so much, will I ever get to see you?'

'No distance is great enough to keep me away from you, my dearest Agnes.'

'Oh, James, you always know the right thing to say. Come, let us sit and feed the ducks. I've brought some bread.'

'I never had you down as an animal lover, Mrs Strome.'

'There are lots of things that you don't know about me, but maybe, if you stick around long enough, rather than running off to sea, you'll get to see what I'm really like.'

'Rest assured, my dear, I have no immediate plans to go off to sea.'

They sat down on a narrow wooden park bench at the edge of the lake, and Mrs Strome took out a small brown paper bag and began to sprinkle breadcrumbs onto the water, attracting a small group of ducks. The atmosphere was pleasant, as children played loudly in the background with their hoops and sticks, and the sweet fragrance from the well-maintained flowerbeds were occasionally picked up and carried by the wind. The couple looked out across the calm, flat lake, and shared a laugh when Walker pointed to a tall, thin man wearing a black top hat on the opposite bank, who appeared to be struggling to stay in the saddle of his bone-shaker bicycle.

'There's so much I don't know about you, too, James,' she said.

'What are you talking about?' he replied. 'You know all there is to know about me.'

'All I know is that your wife died in childbirth three years ago, and that you now live with your brother. Oh, I also know that you never forgave yourself for being away at the time that it happened.'

'There, you see, that's everything. There's nothing more to tell.

'But there is, isn't there?'

'Like what, my love?'

'Like, what did she look like?'

'Who, my wife?'

'Yes, you never talk about her.

'Well, if you must know, she looked very much like you. In fact, if she were here right now, you could pass for sisters.'

'Oh, so that's why you're so attracted to me. I remind you of your dead wife?'

'No, not at all. Though you both may look similar, you are both very different. You're nothing like her.'

'Could you be more specific please?'

'OK, she was shy and timid, and would cry very easily, whereas you, on the other hand, are made of much tougher stuff.'

'So, you think I'm a cold bitch, is that it?'

'What I'm saying is that you're a strong woman, which I like. I like it very much.'

'See, there's still so much we don't know about each other,' she sighed. 'We've only known each other seven months.'

'We've known each other a lot longer than that, my dear.'

'I'm not talking about the times where you visited my husband on business. I mean that it's been seven months to the day since we first made love.'

'Look, Agnes, all you need to know is that I love you very much, and I want to spend the rest of my life with you. What more could you ask of me?'

'Nothing, my love. Nothing at all.'

'And now that you know why I love you, may I ask why you love me?'

'Oh, that's easy. I love you because you're strong and determined. You're nothing like Colin – he's so soft and genteel, and has no backbone. He never takes risks or chances. I find him quite boring, truth be told, whereas you are dangerous and unpredictable, and that's what excites me so.'

'So, you're saying that I'm your diamond in the rough?'

'I'm saying that you're all man, and that's why I love you.'

'The sooner we are married, my dear, the better.'

'Agreed, which brings me to our business here today.'

'Ah yes, old Stowy. It would appear that he has led us on a merry dance, my dear. He had us all fooled playing the dumb mute.'

'Could it really be true that throughout the whole voyage from America to Liverpool, he never uttered a single word?'

'Certainly not in my presence, no. He played the role well.'

'What are we going to do about him, James? He's very close to my husband, and if he should reveal what he knows about us, it will all be over.'

'As I see it, the issue is going to be getting Stowy out of the house where I can kill him.'

'I will lure him out, don't you worry about that. The question is, how will you go about killing him?'

'Slaves end up face-down in the River Mersey every day, my dear. The authorities don't seem to care less.'

'I just want him dead, James. There can be no mistakes.'

'All you have to worry about is getting him out of the house. You can leave the rest to me.'

'Very well. Now, I'd better get back before I'm missed.'

They stood and parted with pecks on the cheek, before walking off in opposite directions.

A small, thin female figure dressed all in black, from her shoes to her large black hat, appeared outside the tradesmen's entrance at the bottom of the stairwell, and tapped lightly on the door.

'Mrs Alsop, there's a Mrs Lamb to see you,' Polly announced.

'Don't just leave her hanging out there,' Mrs Alsop shouted, 'show her in, girl.'

'Yes, Mrs Alsop.'

'Emily,' Mrs Alsop wiped her hands on her apron as she greeted the visitor, 'please have a seat.'

'Thank you, Mary.'

'I'm sorry about Polly. She's a little slow in the head, you understand?'

'Oh, that's quite alright, she's only young.'

'But I wasn't slow,' Polly interrupted. 'I brought Mrs Lamb in right away.'

'Oh, shut up, Polly, and put the kettle on.'

Mrs Alsop had known Mrs Lamb for ten years, and was godmother to her three children, Marcus, Lilly and Rose. The Lambs ran a successful Calico business, and were 'makers of fine gauze and muslin,' as they advertised above the shop doorway.

'Well, this is a pleasant surprise,' Mrs Alsop said. 'How long has it been?'

'Too long, I'm afraid. I see you have a new servant,' Mrs Lamb said, indicating Kwento. 'How long have you had him?

'Oh, not long. The master bought him for a song, I believe. Just ignore him.'

'I must say, he's rather good looking… for one of them, I mean.

'If you say so.'

'Does he speak English?'

'Yes, I do, Mrs Lamb,' Kwento answered.

'Oh, how delightful!'

'Yes, I was educated by missionaries back in Nigeria. Allow me to introduce myself. My name is, Kwento.'

'Well, I'm very pleased to meet you, Kwento. Pray, tell me, Mary, do you think that Mr Strome might possibly consider selling this slave to me?'

Suddenly feeling threatened, Polly positioned herself in front of Kwento.

'Polly!' Mrs Alsop snapped. 'Will you please make Mrs Lamb a nice strong, sweet cup of tea, instead of standing next to darky like a spare part.'

'Sorry, Mrs Alsop,' Polly said in a low voice. 'Would you like a nice strong, sweet cup of tea, too?'

'Yes, why not. Oh, and fetch a plate of my delicious homemade macaroons whilst you're at it.'

'Yes, Mrs Alsop.'

'Um, not for me, thank you,' Mrs Lamb said, holding her hand up in refusal.'

'What?' Mrs Alsop's jaw almost hit the floor. 'No one has ever refused my delicious homemade macaroons.'

'Come now, Mary,' Mrs Lamb said. 'We both know I don't have

a sweet tooth.'

'But… they're not that sweet, Emily.'

'Nevertheless, I must decline.'

Mrs Alsop folded her arms under her ample breasts, clearly miffed by Mrs Lamb's refusal to partake, but she had to put her feelings to one side because she was, after all, still an old friend.

'So, how is everyone?' she asked.

'Well, that's why I've come to see you dressed all in black. Harold passed away last week.'

'Oh, dear Lord, no! He always looked after himself did your Harold. He was as fit as a fiddle.'

'Yes, it came as quite a shock. The children have taken it particularly badly, of course, and as for the family business, well, I fear we may lose everything now.'

'How awful. I'm so sorry for your loss. How did he… if you don't mind me asking?'

'Heart attack,' Mrs Lamb said, taking out a crisp white handkerchief and loudly blowing her nose

'Oh dear.'

'One minute he was standing there larger than life, and then the next he was lying on the living room floor like a beached whale, dead as dead can be.'

Mrs Alsop had always secretly considered Harold Lamb to be a very ugly man, and she could never understand what her friend saw in him, but then she recalled what her dear, sweet mother Ginny used to say.

'There's a poker for every fire, Mary.'

'I just don't know what to say,' she said, drying her eyes on her apron.

'Maybe one of your delicious homemade macaroons might

help?' Polly suggested.

'Go about your business, stupid girl,' Mrs Alsop spat.

'I was only trying to help, Mrs Alsop,' Polly blubbed.

'Just get out,' Mrs Alsop jabbed a pointed finger towards the door. 'You've caused enough trouble already… I'm so sorry about that, Emily. Like I said before, she's a bit retarded, is all.'

'No need to apologise, Mary,' Mrs Lamb said, waving her hands. 'Our hired help acts the very same way. It's the way the youth are today, I'm afraid. Not like in our day, eh?'

'You can say that again. They lack our compassion and empathy, not to mention the pride we take in our work.'

Polly ran out of the room sobbing, with Kwento chasing close behind, just as Bailey was coming the other way.

'Ah, Mr Bailey,' Mrs Alsop brightened. 'You remember Mrs Lamb, don't you?'

'Of course,' Bailey bowed slightly. 'How are you, Mrs Lamb?'

'Her husband's just dropped dead, Mr Bailey.'

'Oh, how unfortunate. My deepest sympathies to you, Mrs. Lamb.

'Yes,' Mrs Alsop continued. 'One minute, he was standing there in the living room, and the next he was hitting the floor like a bloody ton of bricks.'

This frank appraisal set Mrs Lamb off in a fit of uncontrollable weeping, to which Bailey reacted by giving her his handkerchief.

'Come on now, don't go upsetting yourself,' he said. 'Where's Polly gone, Mrs Alsop?'

'Don't mention that girl's name around me,' Mrs Alsop said through gritted teeth. 'I had to send her away for being too insensitive.'

Suddenly, Mrs Lamb jumped up from the table and snatched her bag, before making her excuses under her breath and leaving the same way she came in.

'Emily!' Mrs Alsop shouted after her. 'Where are you going? Come back… was it something I said, Mr Bailey?'

'Um, you might have–'

'Anyway, where's that black rouge got to?'

'I take it you mean Kwento, Mrs Alsop?'

'Isn't that what I just said?'

'He went after Polly, I think.'

'Well, I need him back here to help me.'

'I shall go fetch him.'

As he left, Polly came back in and sat herself down at the table, looking more than a little fed up.

'Well, well, look what the cat's dragged in,' Mrs Alsop tutted. 'You've got some nerve showing up here, after all the trouble you've caused.'

'But I haven't done anything!' Polly protested.

'Haven't done anything? You've only gone and driven off poor old Mrs Lamb. She went out of here like a bat out of hell because of you!

'But–'

'Oh, stop your bleating and make the bitter salad to go with them pigeons, and don't forget to add salt and pepper.

'Yes, Mrs Alsop.

Kwento entered the kitchen holding up his dirty hands, having been handling coal down in the cellar.

'And where the hell have you been?' Mrs Alsop barked.

'I used my initiative and brought up some coal for the fires, Mrs. Alsop,' Kwento answered.

'Initiative? Just swallowed a bloody dictionary, have you? Very well, get yourself cleaned up and then pluck them birds. They won't pluck themselves, you know.'

'Birds?'

'Wood pigeons to you. They're the master's favourite, and he's having them tonight. Don't forget to pluck them upwards, towards the neck.'

'Don't worry, Mrs Alsop,' Kwento grinned, 'I know how to pluck birds. I used to do it back home.'

'And once they've been plucked, give the cavities a good wash and then neatly cut the breasts.'

'Yes, Mrs Alsop.

'Right, I'll leave you to it. I'm taking some of my best hot chicken soup up to Miss Sarah. She's not feeling very well, you see.'

'Oh, I'm sorry to hear that, Mrs Alsop. I hope it's nothing serious.'

Polly did not like hearing Kwento express concern for Miss Sarah, and gave him her most stinging glare.

'Polly, don't forget the walnuts and baby spinach,' Mrs Alsop added. 'I trust I can leave the pair of you on your own?'

'Your wood pigeons are safe with me, Mrs Alsop,' Kwento said.

'It wasn't the pigeons I was talking about,' Mrs Alsop said over her shoulder, as she headed upstairs to Miss Sarah's bedroom.

She knocked lightly on the door before entering to find the young lady lying in bed.

'Hello Miss Sarah,' Mrs Alsop said warmly, 'I've brought you your favourite. A nice bowl of my best hot chicken soup.'

'Oh, Mrs Alsop, you really shouldn't have bothered,' Miss Sarah pulled herself up on her elbows.

'It's no trouble, Miss Sarah. Just a bowl of chicken soup is all.'

'Could you leave it on the sideboard please, Mrs Alsop?'

'Why, what's wrong? Aren't you hungry?'

'I just don't think I could keep it down right now.'

'That's alright, dear,' Mrs Alsop put the tray to one side and then sat herself down next to Miss Sarah on the edge of the bed, and began puffing up her pillow. 'Now, why don't you tell me what's troubling you?'

'Oh, it's nothing really. I just feel a little giddy is all.'

'Miss Sarah, I've been looking after you ever since you were a little baby, and I know when something's wrong. Come on, what's the matter?'

All was going well in the kitchen. Polly had prepared everything she needed for the bitter salad dressing, and was placing various ingredients into small groups on the table: a bowl of vinegar, baby fennel, rocket, raspberries, chicory and, of course, olive oil, but there was something missing. She realised that she had forgot Mrs Alsop's instructions, and was beginning to get herself into a right fluster.

'Polly, are you alright?' Kwento asked.

'No, I can't remember what else Mrs Alsop said. Do you remember?'

'I'm afraid I not. I tend not to listen to her unless I absolutely have to. Why don't you just go upstairs and ask her?'

'I suppose I'll have to, even though she'll no doubt give me a right earful for forgetting. Would you keep an eye on this lot for me?' she indicated the contents of the table.

'Certainly.'

'Alright, I won't be long.'

'Just get going,' he laughed, slapping her squarely on the backside as she went.

Polly climbed the wide staircase that led to the landing outside

Miss Sarah's bedroom door. She was about to knock when she heard raised voices coming from within the bedroom, and she couldn't help but lean forward and put her ear to the door.

'Please will you stop fussing, Mrs Alsop,' Miss Sarah said. 'There's nothing the matter with me!'

'I'll be the judge of that, my girl, and don't you go raising your voice to me!'

'Sorry, Mrs Alsop.'

'Now, I'm going to ask you a question, and I want an honest answer, do you understand?'

'Yes, Mrs Alsop.'

'Are you pregnant?

'How dare you ask me such a thing!'

'Just answer the question, missy.'

'It's none of your damned business if I am or am not.'

'Now you listen to me, young miss, and listen good. If you are pregnant then you're going to need help – my help. So, I'll ask again, are you pregnant?

There was a momentary silence, and then Polly heard Miss Sarah sobbing loudly.

'There, there,' Mrs Alsop said soothingly, 'everything's going to be alright. Mrs Alsop's going to take care of you. Have you told Lieutenant what's-his-name yet?'

'I've been so very stupid, Mrs Alsop,' Sarah wailed. 'I thought he loved me, but then he turned out to be a monster.'

'Most men are, my love, but he's from a very respectable family, and they'll make sure he does right by you.'

'You don't understand, Mrs Alsop. Laurence isn't the father.'

'Oh my. That does complicate matters. Well, if it isn't him, who is it?'

'It's… Barthold.'

'Search the Holly book! You mean Kwento?'

'Yes.'

'Oh, my poor child. Does anyone else know about this?'

'No.'

'Are you sure?'

'Yes, positive. Why?'

'It's just… you do know that you can't keep it, don't you?

'But I want to keep it. You see, Barthold and I are madly in love. We want to get married.'

'You listen here, young lady. You will stop that foolish talk this instant. This union between you and that heathen must end and end now, do you understand?'

'What are you saying, Mrs Alsop?'

'I'm saying that both the slave and the baby will have to go. Now, not a word to anybody else. I will make arrangements for the baby, and then deal with the slave soon after that.'

'When you say "make arrangements," you mean abortion, don't you?'

'Never you mind. For now, just try to get some rest, and I will look in on you later, OK?'

'But, Mrs Alsop–'

'Rest! I will take care of everything.'

'Thank you, Mrs Alsop. You know, I've always considered you to be like a second mother.'

Meanwhile, Polly was rooted to the spot outside Miss Sarah's bedroom door. She was upset, shocked and angry all at the same time. She could just about withstand knowing that Kwento had slept with Miss Sarah, but this latest revelation was too much for her to bear.

How could he do this to me? she thought. He told me that he loves me and wants to marry me, and that we're going to run away together – buy a farm and live out the rest of our lives in peace.

She had revelled in his vision of their shared future, but now, as far as she was concerned, it was one that could never come to pass. Her head was whirling with unanswered questions, like how long had this affair actually been going on for? Was that time she overheard them in the scullery really the first time they had made love? And most importantly, how deep were Kwento's feelings for the beautiful and elegant Miss Sarah?

It felt as though the blood in her brain was reaching boiling point as she turned and dashed back down into the kitchen to confront Kwento, but before she could take him to task, Mrs Alsop was hot on her heels.

'Polly, why haven't you done the seasoning?'

'Because I forgot, Mrs. Alsop.'

'Forgot! What do you mean, forgot? Are you stupid or something?'

Mrs Alsop's timing couldn't have been worse, and Polly, having reached the end of her tether, took hold of a heavy copper saucepan and sent it skimming across the hard, grey stone floor, causing a series of deafening crashes as it went.

'I'm sick and tired of the way you talk to me, Mrs Alsop,' Polly cried, 'and I'll take no more of it, do you hear me?'

'Polly!' Kwento stood in shock at what he was seeing and hearing.

'How dare you speak to me in that manner!' Mrs Alsop barked back.

'Polly, what's wrong?' Kwento asked.

'I overheard Miss Sarah telling Mrs Alsop that she's pregnant with your child,' Polly pointed an accusing finger at Kwento, 'and that you and her are "madly in love" and plan to be married. How could you do this to me, Kwento? I trusted you!'

'Miss Sarah is lying, Polly,' Kwento protested. 'You know that it's you I love, not her.'

'So, is she lying about being pregnant?'

'You've gone too far this time, Polly!' Mrs Alsop interjected. 'You've been eavesdropping, haven't you, you nasty, wicked girl!'

'Please, Mrs Alsop, you're not helping matters,' Kwento said.

'Not helping! You've no idea what I've done for this child, and now look how she repays me. And as for you, you black rogue, you're quite the romancer, aren't you? One woman not enough for you? Just because you can have umpteen wives wherever you come from, doesn't mean that you can do that sort of thing here, me lad-o.'

'Don't you speak to him like that!' Polly exploded. 'I've had enough of you and everyone else in this house. You all think you're better than Kwento and me, but you're not. I know everything that goes on in this house, and you're all hypocrites, the bleeding lot of you!'

'Polly, keep your voice down,' Mrs Alsop whispered.

'Why, are you afraid that all your dirty washing is going to come out next?'

'Polly, please stop this,' Kwento pleaded.

'Oh, let the young madam bury herself,' Mrs Alsop growled.

The growing commotion attracted the attention of Mr Bailey, Mrs Strome and Mr Strome, all of whom entered the kitchen together.

'What's all this, Mrs Alsop?' Mr Strome demanded.

'It's young Polly, sir,' Mrs Alsop said. 'She's gone doolally tap!'

'Polly, what's gotten into you?' Strome asked.

'I've had enough of you all in this bleeding house, sir.'

'Polly, have you gone quite mad?' Strome sounded concerned, but Polly ignored him and instead turned to Kwento.

'Do we have enough money saved?' she asked.

'Um, I think so.'

This made Kwento very uncomfortable, as he knew that Polly was about to reveal their secret plan to Mr Strome. He tried his best to signal to her to stop with his eyes, but she was completely caught up in the moment and could only see red.

'Well?' she persisted. 'Do we or don't we?'

'Yes, I believe we do,' he reluctantly answered.

'What the hell is going on here?' Strome turned his attention to Kwento, who could only lower his head and let his shoulders become rounded, feeling totally dejected in the knowledge that it was all over for him.

'Kwento has saved up enough of your money, Mr Strome, so that we can leave your service,' Polly snarled.

'Who the hell do you think you are?' Mrs Strome roared. 'Fetching off like a demented cow. Remember your place, young lady, and what's all this nonsense about leaving?'

'Maybe you should ask your daughter and Mrs Alsop, mistress,' Polly said. I'm sure they'll tell you all about it.'

'That's enough now, Polly, shut up!' Mrs Alsop jumped in, sounding desperate.

'No, no more "shut up, Polly," or "be quiet, Polly," or "stupid Polly. This time it's you who will shut up, Mrs Alsop!'

'Colin, do something,' Mrs Strome cried. 'This house is out of control.'

'Right, Mr Bailey, clap the slave in irons,' Strome said decisively, 'and as for you, Polly, you're dismissed from this household immediately.'

After a struggle, Bailey managed to physically manhandle Kwento back into his brass neck collar, before marching back into the scullery and chaining him up against the wall.

'Mr Bailey, please take your hands off him,' Polly screamed. 'You can't do that to him!'

'Oh, but I can,' Bailey smirked. 'You're free to leave, Polly, but the slave belongs to the master.'

'So, he's "the slave" again now, not Kwento. I must say, Mr Bailey, that you change sides quicker than Mrs Alsop changes the bleeding menus!'

'I do as I'm told, Polly. Maybe you would still have a job if you did the same.'

'Mummy, Daddy, what's going on?' Miss Sarah announced her presence, looking frail and drained as she gripped the edge of the doorframe for balance.

'It's just Polly, my dear,' Strome said. 'She's gone completely mad.'

'Oh, I'm not mad, sir,' Polly laughed. 'In fact, my mind has never been clearer.'

'Oh, just shut up and get out, you harlot!' Miss Sarah cried.

'Harlot? Ha! That's rich coming from you, Miss Sarah. I'm not the one who's…'

Everything seemed to happen in slow motion. Kwento and Mrs Alsop gasped as they exchanged shocked glances, whilst Polly prepared the big finish that would shake the house to its foundations. She was too emotional to rein herself in, and Kwento knew that what she was about to say could never be unsaid. Polly felt rage and pleasure at the same time, as for the first time in her young life, she was in control, until Strome cut her off mid-flow.

'Be quiet and remember your place, Polly,' he fumed. 'Mrs Alsop, kindly tell me what's happening here?'

'It's like you said, sir, she's not right in the head!'

'Yes, go on, Mrs Alsop,' Polly taunted, 'blacken my name to save your own.'

'I've no idea what you're talking about, you stupid girl.'

'Really? What about the affair that you and Mr Bailey have been having. And you, a married woman and all.'

'I've been separated from my husband for more than twenty years,' Mrs Alsop fired back, using the back of a chair to steady herself. 'Not that it's any of your business, mind.'

'Polly, this is outrageous,' Strome said firmly.

'You mean you didn't know, sir? They've been at it for better part of twelve months. I heard them creeping around, in and out of each other's bedrooms every night.'

'Colin, flog this bitch and then throw her out onto the street where she belongs,' Mrs Strome erupted. 'She's nothing more than a common guttersnipe, fit for nothing but being trampled on.'

'If I'm a guttersnipe, what does that make you, mistress? I mean, with all that you've been getting up to recently.'

'What the hell is she talking about, Agnes?' Strome looked accusingly at his wife.

'I've no idea, Colin,' Mrs Strome lowered her eyes. 'She's completely lost the plot.'

'Oh, I am sorry, mistress,' Polly said, hands on hips, 'you must have forgot?

'You spiteful, horrid little child! Oh my, I think I'm going to faint.'

Mrs Strome began wafting her hand in front of her face, before she fell into an empty chair and then shielded her eyes, as though fending off an episode.

'Polly, really, what is the meaning of all this?' Mr Strome asked pleadingly.

'I didn't start any of it, Mr Strome, but I intend to be the one to finish it. All I wanted was for Kwento and me to live out the rest of our lives in peace. Was I asking too much?'

In yet another unexpected turn of events, Polly herself collapsed to the hard floor. Mrs Alsop moved to tend to her, while all Kwento could do was watch helplessly from the scullery doorway. He had never experienced anything so terrible in all his life, not even during his worst times in the Americas. At least then, he still had hope of a better future, but that would no longer be the case now that his plan to finally become master of his own destiny had been exposed before the time was right.

'Is she alright, Mrs Alsop?' Strome asked. 'Do we need to send for a doctor?'

'She's alright, Mr Strome,' Mrs Alsop said. 'No need for a doctor.'

'Are you sure, Mrs Alsop? She looks rather pale.

'She's pregnant is all, sir.

Just when Kwento thought things couldn't get any worse, that's exactly what happened. All eyes were now upon him once again, as he backed away deeper into the scullery and sat down on his cot, head in hands, totally drained.

'Good God!' Strome exclaimed. 'Is there something in the drinking water? Mr Bailey, carry Polly up to bed whilst my wife and I try to sort out this horrid mess.'

'Yes, sir.'

'No,' Mrs Alsop cut in. 'Leave her be, Mr Bailey. I'll look after her.'

'Are you sure, Mrs Alsop?' Strome said doubtfully.

'She'll be just fine with me, sir.

'Very well.'

The room began to empty out in stunned silence, except for Polly, Mrs Alsop and Kwento, who was still chained to the scullery wall.

Polly was sitting at the kitchen table, drying her eyes with Mrs Alsop's white handkerchief while occasionally glancing across at Kwento, who was still on his cot with his head lowered, staring down at the floor, avoiding eye contact. She knew that he would be angry at her for not stopping her tirade when he had silently implored her to, but that was by the bye now, as she had finally realised the enormity of what she had done. Not only that, but she deeply regretted it.

'Thank you, Mrs Alsop,' she said, handing back the damp handkerchief. 'What do you think will happen now? I've upset so many people.'

'To be honest, Polly, I don't know,' Mrs Alsop shrugged, 'but what I do know is that the master is a fair and kind man, and I have faith that he will make the right decision. Now, get this nice cup of strong, sweet tea down your neck.'

Polly took a big gulp and did her best to force a smile, only for one glance across at Kwento to leave her feeling miserable again.

'I'm so sorry, Kwento,' she said. 'I fear I've messed everything up for the both of us. Can you find it in your heart to forgive me?'

'Of course I forgive you,' Kwento replied quietly. 'I could never stay angry with you. You did what you felt you had to do, and as for what happens next, it's like Mrs Alsop says. Everything rests with the master now.'

'Oh, my dearest Kwento, we were so close to being away from this place, if only I'd kept my big mouth shut. I fear that I have lost you forever now.'

'Don't be silly, you haven't lost me at all. I will be with you forever, my love. We must stay positive, and we must be strong, for the sake of our child if nothing else.'

'Oh, so you admit that you're the father, then?' Mrs Alsop said.

'Of course I'm the father! I intend to do the right thing by both Polly and the baby, no matter what.'

'There you see, Polly, everything's going to be alright,' Mrs Alsop cheered. 'Now, enough of all this negative talk. Finish you cup of nice strong, sweet tea, there's a good girl.'

That was when the Stromes and their daughter entered the kitchen, accompanied by Bailey.

'Mr Bailey,' Strome said, 'kindly unshackle the slave please.

'Yes, sir.'

'Excuse me, Mr Strome, what's going on?' Mrs Alsop asked.

'Because the slave is my property, he will be staying on,' Strome answered. 'As for the rest of you, you must leave this house.'

'But we've done nothing wrong, sir,' Mrs Alsop protested.

Agnes stepped forward with a smirk on her face.

'You've all conspired to bring this house into disrepute,' she said, 'and now you must leave.'

'That's not true, mistress,' Polly cried. 'We've given you nothing but good service.'

'Oh, this is pointless,' Agnes threw up her hands. 'We're just going around in circles. You're all fired, now get out!'

'Mummy, no,' Miss Sarah stepped in front of her mother, 'you can't throw Mrs Alsop out onto the street like a common peasant. She's been like a mother to me!'

'Don't waste your breath, Miss Sarah,' Mrs Alsop shook her head knowingly. 'This has been coming for a long time, hasn't it, Mrs Strome?'

'I'm sure I don't know what you're talking about.'

'You've always resented the bond between Miss Sarah and me, ever since she was born.'

'Oh, stop blathering, you silly old woman, and get out.'

'I'm going alright, but not before I've had my say. You were only too happy to hand Miss Sarah over to me when she was a baby because looking after her was too much trouble for you, but now that she's all grown up and can look after herself, you suddenly want her back.'

'I don't have to listen to this twaddle. You and your little gang have brought this house into disrepute, and I'll not have you here a moment longer. Colin, will you please do something!'

'I'm sorry, Mrs Alsop, but you have to leave,' Strome said, unable to look the woman in the eye as he spoke to her.'

'Before I do, may I say something to you, and you alone?'

Strome gave a short nod.

'In all the years I've worked for you, have I ever asked you for anything?'

'No, Mrs Alsop. You have not.'

'Well, I'm asking now, sir. In fact, I'm begging you, please don't put Polly out onto the streets. She's just a child, and a very silly one at that.'

Strome paced up and down the kitchen floor with one hand behind his back and the other hand on his chin, all the while glancing across at his wife, who he feared would explode at any minute if he didn't go along with her. Then, however, he made a shocking decision to take a stand against her, to show her that he wasn't the weak, indecisive invertebrate that she had always made him out to be.

'Agreed,' he said.

'Oh, thank you, sir,' Mrs Alsop beamed.

'Colin!'

'Do not interfere please, darling,' Strome turned to face his wife. 'This is my house, and I've decided that they're all going to stay on.

'Colin!'

'I think we should retire, my dear. We have much to discuss.

With that, Strome took her by the arm and led her out of the kitchen, followed quickly by Miss Sarah and Bailey, leaving Polly, Mrs Alsop and Kwento to stare at each other in amazement. Mrs Alsop placed her arms around her and gave her a big hug.

Agnes, still reeling from her most recent defeat at the hands of her husband, now decided to direct her attention towards Mrs Alsop. On the surface, the mistress of the house appeared calm, but beneath the cold exterior was a raging fire, and she was out for revenge. Nobody was safe, as in her mind, her husband had belittled her in front of the staff.

She approached Mrs Alsop and offered her deepest apologies, claiming that her outburst was merely a moment of madness, and that she agreed with her husband's decision completely. However, this sudden change in demeanour only served to fuel Mrs Alsop's suspicions further, leaving her even more curious about what was to come next, and she wouldn't have to wait long to find out.

Agnes began to probe on the matter of her daughter's delicate condition, but Mrs Alsop resisted her charm offensive, so much so that a change of tack was required, as she went through her full arsenal of deceptive tactics. It took quite some time, but Mrs Alsop eventually broke down and told Agnes that Kwento had got Miss Sarah pregnant, before explaining that she was in the process of organising an abortion.

Satisfied at last, Agnes swore Mrs Alsop to secrecy, instructing her to do nothing and to say nothing, adding that she would be the one to arrange an abortion. Then, armed with this new information, she went straight to her daughter and told her that if she didn't go along with everything she was about to hear, she would tell her father the truth about her and the slave, telling the girl in no uncertain terms that this would lead to her being disowned by her father, and possibly even put out on to the streets.

Sarah agreed without needing to hear what the plan was, after which Agnes set her sights on Kwento. She bided her time with this one, waiting to get him on his own before delivering her ultimatum, which involved confronting him with a warning that if her husband were to find out the truth about his liaison with Sarah, it would destroy the business arrangement between them. She demanded that he leave the house immediately, only for Kwento to point out that he was not a free man, and thus could not leave 19 Folly Fields of his own accord.

Thinking on her feet, Agnes offered to seek out a solicitor and draft a contract of ownership that he could then buy back from her, giving him his freedom. She could do this because she knew that her husband had paid cash for him, but had declined to keep the receipt, thinking such a thing to be indecent. As payment, Kwento would provide her with sound advice on the sugarcane industry, enabling her to go into business for herself and become a woman of independent means. She recalled overhearing him tell her husband that whilst he was on the Marion plantation, a group of slaves had been brought across to America from St Kitts and Nevis for the purpose of instructing the American slaves on how to plant and process sugarcane, and how he had spent quite some time with them before they were shipped off across the deep south, during which time his knowledge of the sugar refinement industry grew exponentially. She then explained how she had always wanted to go into the refinement business, but that her husband had flatly refused to even talk about it.

Kwento didn't seemed swayed by the offer, and so Agnes turned the screw on him one last time, warning that she would go to the police and have him charged with the rape of her daughter, and asking what he thought the chances were that they would accept his word over hers. Realising that he was beaten, Kwento slumped against the cold, damp wall of the scullery, and Agnes smirked as she handed him a pencil and paper, on which he was to write a list of the best sugar plantations to invest in, before collecting the money he'd saved and leaving the house that very night, but what Kwento could not know was that once out of the house, he would fall prey to Captain Walker's murderous plan to get rid of him.

As he crept out on to the street, Kwento stopped to look back at the house. His heart was heavy and his head was spinning, as he wondered what would happen to his dear, sweet Polly, whilst he roamed the streets until he found the Turk's Head tavern, a public house in the city centre, where he managed to secure lodgings.

The Turk's Head was a den of iniquity frequented by sailors, gangsters and prostitutes, a place where the wrong look might see you get your throat cut. The proprietor, a Mrs Doris Boyd, was a rotund woman with a sharp nose and a hard, powdered white face, with thin, brightly-painted red lips. Her deep lines were the marks of a very hard life, but she had taken a liking to poor Kwento and treated him kindly, offering him a tiny attic room that he eagerly accepted. Being no stranger to hardship himself, these dangers did not bother Kwento in the least. In fact, he thought the tavern to be quite tame compared to the harsh, hot plains of the Savannah cotton fields back in America.

The following morning, the staff at 19 Folly fields woke to find that Kwento was missing. Mr Strome was left furious and feeling betrayed, whilst Polly was completely heartbroken and inconsolable, despite Mrs Alsop's best efforts. Needless to say, the mood in the house was sombre, save for Agnes, who could barely contain her excitement as she sent Captain Walker a letter with instructions to meet in Sefton Park. There, they finalised the murder plot, leaving no stone unturned, as she declared that her husband should be killed right there in the same spot the following night, next to the old Palm House, rather than at the Coburg Dock as suggested by Captain Walker. She told Walker that her husband and daughter would arrive under the pretence of meeting Bernard Miles, father of Sarah's fiancé Laurence, who had a mansion nearby, in order to discuss wedding arrangements. However, upon reaching the bench where the 'meeting' would be held, they would find Walker waiting to receive them. Sarah would be wearing a long pearl neckless, to make it easier for Walker to identify her in the dark, which he would take after throttling Strome, giving the appearance of a robbery gone wrong. Finally, Sarah would provide the police with a description that would have them searching the streets for a young African male who looked awfully like a certain slave who had recently left her father's service.

Captain Walker agreed in principle that it was indeed a good plan and that it could work, but he had just one reservation: he wanted to know how Agnes had swayed her daughter into going along with it. At this, Agnes laughed before giving a brief outline of what had happened in the house, and how it led to the shock announcement of the two pregnancies. She went on to say that she had promised her daughter an abortion and a share of her husband's life insurance payout upon confirmation of his death, allowing her to protect her honour, marry Lieutenant Miles and see out her days in the Caribbean.

The bar at the Turk's Head Kwento was beginning to fill up when Kwento returned after paying a small deposit on a croft on the outskirts of the city. He was very excited, and couldn't wait to return to 19 Folly Fields and break the good news to Polly, but as he ascended the narrow attic staircase that led to his rented room, he overheard a familiar voice speaking quietly at a table just below his feet. Crouching down, he listened as Captain Walker bragged to a group of his cronies about how, at ten o'clock that night, he was going to ambush some rich gent and his daughter outside the old Palm House, after which he would claim the man's wife and wealth for himself. As if that wasn't shocking enough, he then revealed his plan to kill the wife once the dust had settled, before taking her money and returning to sea.

Being in no doubt as to whom Walker was referring, Kwento crept up the staircase and quietly locked himself inside his room, where he meditated on the fact that Captain Walker was far more devious and dangerous than Agnes could ever be.

The moon shone bright and clear against the black sky, casting silvery, ghostly shadows across the slowly swaying oak trees, and Miss Sarah could see her own breath rising in the damp air as she walked arm in arm with her father, nervously playing with her long pearl neckless as they went. In the near distance, she could just make out a dark figure sitting on a park bench next to the old Palm House, exactly as her mother had described. Her heart began to pound in her chest like a big bass drum as they got nearer and nearer to the target, until it became too much and she pulled back sharply on her father's arm.

'What's the matter, Sarah?' Strome asked.

'Daddy, don't go over there,' she pleaded.

'What's got into you,' he laughed, 'it's only Bernard. There's nothing to be afraid of.'

'No, Daddy, please stop.'

She gasped as the dark figure suddenly rose to his feet and pulled back his hood, before stepping out from the shadows and revealing himself.

'Good God, man!' Strome cried. 'Kwento, what on earth are you doing here, and where is Bernard Miles?'

'Sir, I'm here because there was a plot to murder you this very night,' Kwento answered.

'Murder? Who would want to murder me?'

'Captain Walker, sir.'

'Why would Captain Walker plot to murder me? You're not making any sense, man!'

'What I'm telling you is the truth, sir. Your daughter can confirm it.'

'It's true, Daddy,' Sarah said, her head lowered.'

'You mean to say that you knew about this?' Strome looked accusingly at his daughter.

'It's not entirely Miss Sarah's fault, sir,' Kwento said.

'How's that, then?'

'I believe she was manipulated by her mother, sir. Am I correct in that assumption, Miss Sarah?'

'Yes, that's correct,' Sarah began to weep. 'Oh, I'm so sorry, Daddy.

'Do you seriously expect me to believe that my wife could do something like this?' Strome barked. 'It's outrageous!'

At that point, Kwento sat Strome and his daughter down on the same bench where he'd waited for them, and began to recount everything he knew, including his own affair with Miss Sarah, which she in turn corroborated. Naturally, Strome was shocked by what he was hearing, and he continued to find it difficult to accept his wife's involvement in the murder plot. This prompted Kwento to suggest that they all make their way to the Turk's Head tavern to confront Captain Walker and discover the awful truth.

With Sarah's encouragement, Strome reluctantly agreed, and no sooner had they entered the tavern than they happened across Captain Walker alone at a table, drunk. The sailor looked stunned to find Strome standing before him, and carefully placed his drink down on the table before speaking.

'The fact that you're here tells me that you know everything, sir,' he said.

'Indeed,' Strome nodded, 'but I need to know one more thing.'

'Ask, and I shall answer honestly.'

'Is it true that my wife was involved in this hideous affair?'

'She was more than involved,' Walker laughed bitterly. 'She organised the whole thing. I'm very glad that Stowy intervened before the deed could be done. Really, I am.'

'Stowy?'

'He's referring to me, sir,' Kwento said.

'Whatever the case, I've heard enough,' Strome shook his head in disgust. 'Come, let's be away from here.'

Back at 19 Folly Fields, it was ten minutes past midnight and Agnes was nervously pacing the floor, waiting for Sarah and the police to knock with the terrible news of her husband's death. In her head, she kept rehearsing how she would break down in front of the constables, until finally there came three dull knocks at the front door. She then listened for Mr Bailey's light footsteps coming up from the kitchen, as she turned to the large, ornate mirror mounted on the wall and began to stroke her long auburn hair with trembling hands, in an attempt at psyching herself up ahead of what would have to be the performance of her life.

Moments later, the living room door swung open as, to her great surprise, Bailey led Kwento into the room, followed closely by her husband and daughter.

'The game is up, my dear,' Strome declared, before his wife could so much as utter a word. 'Kwento has told me everything.'

'I'm sure I don't know what you're talking about,' Agnes replied, determined to keep her cool.

'I'm talking about the murder plot that you and your lover, Captain Walker, hatched together. Like I said, Kwento has told me everything.'

'And you believe him, do you?

'At first, I did not, but then he provided me with some very compelling evidence. Oh, and that reminds me. Mr Bailey, fetch the brass neck collar, would you? There's a good chap.

'Yes, sir,' Bailey nodded.

Kwento froze with fear at the thought of being chained up again, but did not give any outward reaction beyond a sideways glance at Strome, who he realised was not aware of the deal that had been struck between his wife and his slave in regard to the contract of ownership.

'You would take the word of a fucking slave over that of your own wife?' Agnes spat, eyes aflame with incredulity.

'It's not just Kwento's word, Mummy,' Sarah interjected. 'I also told Daddy everything I knew.'

'Oh, you Judas – you Jezebel!' Agnes ranted. 'Stabbed in the back by my own flesh and blood. How could you?'

'That's quite enough,' Strome said calmly. 'Mr Bailey, please place the collar on Mrs Strome, and then chain her to the scullery wall.'

'Sir?' Bailey said, visibly uncomfortable.

'Just do as I say.

'Yes, sir.'

Bailey seized Agnes by the arm, tightening his grip as she struggled trying to pull away whilst he forced her towards the door.

'Wait, Mr Bailey,' Kwento called after him. 'I need to speak with Mrs Strome.'

Bailey looked to Mr Strome, who nodded his assent.

'Do you have my contract?' Kwento asked her.

'No, I do not,' Agnes sneered. 'Did you really believe that I was going to set you free?'

'But you promised!'

'Have you never heard the saying, a promise is only a comfort to a fool?'

Unfortunately, he had heard it before, and now it sent a cold shiver down his spine as he remembered way back to his time aboard the Douglas. He also remembered Baku's wise words, which Akin chose to ignore to his own detriment.

Kwento's heart sank as he realised that he had learnt nothing from his horrendous experiences, and wondered how he could have allowed himself to be tricked into this position.

'Contract? Strome asked. 'What contract?'

'I gave your wife some of my savings, sir, in order to buy my freedom,' Kwento admitted. 'I also used some of the money to put down a small deposit on a croft on the outskirts of the city. The rest I used to pay Captain Walker to leave the country.'

Upon hearing this, Agnes became hysterical and started to scream, as on top of everything else that had happened, the thought of losing the love of her life was too much to bear.

Strome repeated the order for Bailey to confine his wife to the scullery, before turning to face Kwento.

'Am I to understand that you have no savings left?'

'That is correct, sir. I'm afraid all is lost for me now. I remain in your service, and at your mercy.'

'Perhaps not,' Strome smiled.

'Excuse me, sir?'

'I will refund all that you have paid to my wife and Captain Walker, and you are to be formally released from my possession.'

'I – I don't understand, sir.'

'You used your own money to save my life, and the only way I can possibly repay that debt is by giving you yours. You are a free man, Kwento.'

The following morning, Kwento and Polly left 19 Folly Fields together, to live out the rest of their lives in the countryside. Meanwhile, Captain Walker had already set sail for Barbados, never to be seen in Britain again, and Miss Sarah agreed to give evidence against her mother, who was later arrested and charged with attempted murder. Sarah never did marry Lieutenant Laurence Miles, instead choosing to remain in her father's house, where she raised her child with the help of Mrs Alsop and Mr Bailey, who were both now a confirmed and very happy couple.

As for Kwento, he would never forget the day he held Polly's hand as he walked her along the long, winding, narrow country lane that led to the old brown thatched croft for the first time. The clouds were grey and heavy, and darkness was about to descend as he pointed over towards a large, overgrown field to the right of the croft.

'See that field, Polly,' he said proudly, 'that's ours.'

Approaching a small, off-white picket fence, Kwento, being ever the gentleman, leaned forward to unlatch the gate for future wife, only for the rotted old wood to fall apart in his hands. They both laughed long and loud at this, and then he scooped her up into his arms, kicked open the front door and carried her over the threshold.

THE SUN GOES UP, THE SUN GOES DOWN

The master frowns high in the saddle with whip unfurled, no pity for the soul, only passion for the work and the brown heavy soil. Then, the crack of the whip fills the heart with dread, another crack turns the black to red. Babies cry and mother's weep, cradled on breast, no food to eat.

The sun goes up, the sun goes down.

Sixteen-hour days, no parole, no reprieve, with all hope lost, no shoes on their feet. In his eyes we are lazy, bestial and weak, born into slavery, death the only release. Work to the beat in the bright searing heat.

The sun goes up, the sun goes down.

Lee Knafa

BIBLIOGRAPHY

Most of the material relating to slavery in this book was sourced from the 1992 published papers by Mr Wilson Carlton Eugene PhD of the University of North Carolina at Chapel Hill, and from Dicky Sam's Liverpool and Slavery, an historical account of the Liverpool-African slave trade, both of which were provided by Patricia Jonker Cholwe BSc Hons, the University of Liverpool. There is also a quotation from the Douay-Rheims Bible, First Book of Machabees, Chapter One. Any other material used in this book is from the author's own memories.

All characters in this book, except those named below, are entirely fictitious. Any similarity to actual persons living or dead is purely coincidental:

Captain Luck Collingwood
Governor Sir Charles McCarthy
Ira Aldridge (actor)
George Frederick Cook (actor)
Ellen Turner

Edward Wakefield
Edward Thevenot
Margaret Daulby

Dedicated to all the enslaved and displaced Africans taken from the areas listed below:

Benue
Akwa
Ibom
Kogi
Kano
Jigawa
Borno
Edo
Kwara
Whydah
Niger
Bissau
Gabon
Congo
Angola
Benin
Senegal
Gambia
Bissau
Sierra Leon
Liberia
Ghana
Congo
Angola

Mozambique
Madagascar

Printed in Great Britain
by Amazon

14967357R00112